"We have to find th...

But before she'd taken more than a couple of steps, the officer wrapped his big hand around her wrist to stop her.

"You need to go outside, Miss Potter," he told her. "I will search the home."

She tugged her wrist away. "But the baby could be hurt—"

"I will find him," he said, his deep voice almost vibrating with the vow. It wasn't exactly a promise, though—more like grim determination.

Was he worried, like she was, that he would find the baby the same way they'd found Ella?

"You need to step outside, Miss Potter," he said. "This is a crime scene." He pointed at the door. His hand was steady, though. As steady as he seemed despite what they'd found.

She, meanwhile, was shaken, and not just over Ella, but Simon, too. Where was he?

"Look for the baby," she said before she pushed open the door and stepped onto the first of the wooden steps. The sole of her shoe slipped on the weathered wood, and she had to reach out and grasp the railing before she fell. As she steadied herself, she noticed a bright speck of blue in the overgrown bushes beside those stairs. Blue yarn, knitted together to form a baby's bootie, but the blue yarn was stained with blood...

New York Times and *USA TODAY* bestselling, award-winning author **Lisa Childs** has written more than eighty-five novels. Published in twenty countries, she's also appeared on the *Publishers Weekly*, Barnes & Noble and Nielsen Top 100 bestseller lists. Lisa writes contemporary romance, romantic suspense, paranormal and women's fiction. She's a wife, mom, bonus mom, avid reader and less avid runner. Readers can reach her through Facebook or her website, lisachilds.com.

BABY RESCUE MISSION

LISA CHILDS

LOVE INSPIRED
INSPIRATIONAL ROMANCE

LOVE INSPIRED®
INSPIRATIONAL ROMANCE

Recycling programs
for this product may
not exist in your area.

ISBN-13: 978-1-335-46840-6

Baby Rescue Mission

Love Inspired
22 Adelaide St. West, 41st Floor
Toronto, Ontario M5H 4E3, Canada
www.LoveInspired.com

Printed in U.S.A.

Though I walk in the midst of trouble,
thou wilt revive me: thou shalt stretch forth
thine hand against the wrath of mine enemies,
and thy right hand shall save me.
—*Psalm* 138:7

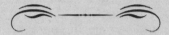

For my daughter Ashley Renae,
my inspiration for so many of the strong,
smart heroines I write but most especially
for this heroine, Renae.

As a child protective services investigator,
Ashley works so hard to protect those who
cannot protect themselves. She is the "right hand"
and an amazing person!

ONE

"Help me...please, help me..."

The voice, little louder than a whisper, emanated from the speaker on Renae Potter's work cell phone, the one used exclusively for her job as a Child Protective Services investigator. The plea surprised her. In her seven years on the job, she'd heard more people deny that they needed help than she'd had people ask for it.

"Who is this?" Her question echoed inside the vehicle the State Department provided for her to use during an investigation.

She was on the road trying to track down a child whose teacher had reported concerns that her student was being neglected at home. The parents must have known that report was coming because they hadn't sent their child to school today, though that might have been because of their neglect. They also hadn't answered their phone or their doorbell. From the number of cars parked in the gravel driveway, she suspected they might have been home, but she couldn't force them to open their door. And she had no grounds to involve the police yet, since the teacher had confirmed there were no signs of physical abuse on the student. Renae had tucked her card in their screen door. Maybe the child had found it.

After steering the vehicle onto the gravel shoulder of the highway, she put the transmission into Park, pushed her curly dark hair over her shoulder and focused on her phone. The number on the screen wasn't in her contacts, so she had no idea to whom it belonged, just that it had the same area code as her work phone, so it was also in Coral County in northern Michigan.

"Help me," the voice murmured again.

Maybe the little girl had found her card in the door. But even though the voice was faint and hard to understand, Renae didn't think it belonged to someone as young as the first grader she was looking for.

"How can I help you?" she asked. That was what she wanted most, was why she'd gone into this field. She wanted to help people who needed help. Something she wished she'd been able to do long ago.

"Going…to kill me," the voice rasped out of the speaker in a disjointed whisper. "If I don't…give up my baby."

"Who's going to kill you?" she asked, her pulse beginning to pound fast and fierce, as fear gripped her. Fear for her caller and the child. "Are you in immediate danger?"

"Yes."

Alarm shot through her. "We need to call nine-one-one—"

"Too late."

"No, tell me where you are," Renae beseeched the woman. "Tell me who you are. I'll get help. I'll come—"

"Too late for me," the voice interjected again.

Despite how soft the raspy whisper was, it sounded faintly familiar. Since the young woman had Renae's cell-phone number, they had probably talked before. Unless she'd gotten the number off Renae's business card that she handed out while doing interviews or when she was looking to track down someone, like the one she'd just left in the screen door of the first grader's house.

"Who are you?" she asked again.

"Save my baby...please. He's... He's..." The faint voice trailed off.

"He's where?" Renae prodded. "Where are *you*? I need to know where you—" The soft hum of static was gone as the line went completely dead and the call was lost. Renae worried that the caller might be as well. At least lost to her...

She pressed the number on the screen, trying to call it back, but got the service provider message: *This call cannot be completed at this time.*

Was it the woman's phone? Was she out of range?

Renae's worked when, desperate to help the woman, she placed her own emergency call to 911, identified herself and explained what had just happened. "We need to find this woman right away."

"I'm trying to reach the number you gave me," the dispatcher said, "but the phone must be dead. I'm just getting the message from the service provider."

"Can you somehow locate the cell phone?" With how poor the reception had been, the young woman must have been using one. Or her voice could have cut in and out because she was injured and struggling to stay conscious. "She might need an ambulance, too. She's in grave danger. And she has a baby."

The young woman had said *he* when she'd asked Renae to protect him. She had a baby boy. Finally, Renae realized why the voice had sounded familiar. She'd recently interviewed the young woman. Ella…

"Ella Sedlecky!" she exclaimed. "That's who it was." Someone had called CPS on the single mother with the complaint that the nineteen-year-old was leaving her infant alone while she worked and entertained men. They'd also accused Ella of abusing drugs.

Ella had willingly submitted to a drug test, which had come back clean of all substances. With home visits, pediatrician reports and interviews with people who knew Ella, Renae had thoroughly investigated the claim and had found no evidence of neglect or inappropriate behavior on the part of the young mother. The complainant who'd called Child Protective Services had refused to identify themselves or provide any corroborating evidence to support the statement they'd refused to make in person. The number that had called in the complaint had been traced back to a pay-as-you-go cell.

Unfortunately CPS received too many calls like that from people just trying to make trouble for other people, and CPS and the police departments were stretched too thin to pursue the prank callers. Renae had asked Ella if she knew who might have reported her, but the young mother had claimed to have no idea. Renae had tried to question the woman's ex-husband, who'd filed for divorce when his young wife had told him she was pregnant. He'd wanted nothing to do with Ella or their son, who he claimed wasn't his.

Even though Ella had told Renae that she hadn't cheated, she hadn't wanted to force her ex to take a paternity test. She hadn't wanted any involvement with him.

That had concerned Renae. She'd thought that Ella's ex may have threatened her, but the young woman had insisted she wasn't in danger and that nobody was threatening her or her baby. But now…

That person must have showed themselves to Ella. And maybe even hurt her?

"I need an officer and…" Her voice cracked, but she had to consider the reason why that call had dropped. "Have an ambulance meet me at…" She opened her laptop and frantically typed in Ella's name to pull up the report. The report she'd closed at the conclusion of her thirty-day investigation a month ago. She shouldn't have closed it before she identified the person who made the anonymous report, before she found whoever had tried to make trouble for the young mother who was already struggling to raise a child all on her own. But when the number couldn't be traced, and Ella had had no ideas, Renae had been forced to move on to new cases, to protect kids that were genuinely in danger. Ella's little boy had been safe, or so Renae had believed.

Please, God, help me help her and her son.

"Here's the address I have for her." Renae read off the street number and name from Ella's case file. "I'm not that far away."

"Miss Potter, you have to wait for police," the dispatcher advised. "You can't go there alone."

It was as if she knew exactly what Renae was thinking. Knew about the urge tearing her apart inside...

Please, God, make sure that Ella and her baby are all right.

"Maybe the phone just died," Renae said, then panic clutched her, pressing on her lungs as she considered the horrible alternative—that the young mother might be dead. "Or she lost the cell signal. That could be the reason the call ended. Maybe she's totally fine." She wanted to convince herself of that as much as she wanted to convince the dispatcher.

Please, God, let it be true—let her and the baby be okay.

But Renae had a horrible feeling that no matter how fervently she prayed, it was too late for her prayer for Ella to be answered.

"Because she admitted to being in danger, you cannot go out to her house alone," the dispatcher continued. "You need to wait for the police to arrive and make sure it's safe before you start any of your interviews."

As a Child Protective Services investigator, Renae spent a lot of time doing interviews, talking to kids, parents, witnesses—determining the level of the threat, or if there even was one. How had she missed this one?

Because of the anonymous complaint, she'd been looking for the threat that the young mother posed to her four-week-old baby, but she hadn't found one. She'd found instead a young woman who fiercely loved her baby and wanted to provide for him and protect him.

Now she realized she should have tried harder to find out who had called in that complaint to CPS. Maybe they had been the real threat.

Although often times in situations like this, the caller was just some busybody or a jealous ex, Ella had insisted that her ex hadn't been jealous, that he'd just wanted nothing to do with her and their baby, and she was too proud to force him.

Ella had been determined to take care of her baby and herself all on her own, supporting them with the wages and tips from her waitressing job at a restaurant in the nearby inland lake community of Coral Creek. The northern Michigan town was popular for fishing in the summer and hunting in the winter. But even with her tips and an inheritance from her grandfather, Ella had been struggling to support herself and her child.

Renae had tried to help them out with a referral to the financial assistance department of Human Services to get help with expenses like food and utilities and childcare. After meeting with Ella and interviewing the people who knew her, Renae had figured that the only real help the young mother had needed had been financial.

Not this kind of help. Not protection from danger.

The dispatcher's voice emanated from the cell speaker. "The closest available unit is a state trooper. His name is Sergeant Mayweather."

Since transferring to this county a few months ago, Renae had gotten to know some of the state police officers, but that name didn't ring a bell.

"How close is he?" Renae asked. She typed the address from the report into her cell's maps app. The address was for a mobile home that had been part of Ella's inheritance, an old fishing "cabin" that her grandfather had retired to and where he'd raised Ella after her single mother died in a traffic accident.

"Fifteen minutes." The voice came from the app on Renae's phone, not from the dispatcher.

"Twenty," the dispatcher said, but she was obviously referring to how long it would take the state trooper to reach the address Renae had given her. "You need to wait for Sergeant Mayweather, Miss Potter."

Five minutes...

With a child in danger, those five minutes might be critical. They could be the difference between life and death. If he was left alone, he could choke on something, aspirate or, if he wasn't alone, he might be in even more danger.

Ella's last words to Renae echoed in her mind. *Save my baby.*

Frantic with worry for him and his mother, Renae quickly skimmed through the report on her laptop, trying to find the baby's name. Simon Sedlecky.

Ella had named her baby after her beloved grandfather, and when Renae had interviewed her a month ago, the young woman had made it very clear how much she'd loved her baby, so very much that she would do whatever she could for him. If he was in danger, like his mother feared, Renae had to do whatever she could to save him, even if she had to break protocol.

When the radio call came in, Clark was farther away than he would have been if he hadn't had an emergency of his own and had to sign out of service for a couple of hours. With his mom in the hospital from a fall at his house, he would have taken a personal day for the rest of the day—should have—but the local police post was already short-staffed. His mother, knowing that he was needed on patrol, had insisted he didn't need to stay, that between his stepdad and her sister, she had everything covered. But leaving her and his young daughter…

While leaving them had been hard for him to do, it didn't compare to what he'd done two years ago… when he'd buried his wife. His mom's broken ankle wasn't that serious, but he was still shaken over her getting hurt, especially because she'd been alone with his daughter at the time. Hopefully, this call was nothing, just a social worker being overly cautious.

He didn't blame her. Miss Potter. That was the name the dispatcher had given him. He hadn't met her before, but then he'd only been back on the road for a few weeks. After working as an instructor at the nearby state police training center the past two years, he'd been asked to resume patrol duties a few weeks ago due to the department being so short-handed. Miss Potter had probably started with Child Protective Services after Clark had made the switch to instructor.

CPS investigators tended to come and go, either because they got burned out with all the emotions and frustrations of trying to protect kids, or they got scared off because of the threats. Their job was sometimes more dangerous than his. At least he could carry a weapon and defend himself from an attack. CPS workers weren't allowed to carry firearms or even pepper spray during their investigations. If they suspected they would be in danger during an interview or home visit, they had to request law enforcement to accompany them. To protect them.

Some were understandably cautious, while others took risks they shouldn't. Risks like his late wife had taken. But Ann had been a police officer; she'd been armed and able to defend herself. She just hadn't had time. The minute she'd stepped out of her vehicle to respond to a domestic-violence call, the suspect had fired at her, striking her in the head. She'd died immediately there in a driveway, while her backup had taken cover as the suspect fired at them before turning the gun on himself.

Clark's heart ached, as it always did, when he thought of her, of the wonderful woman he'd lost. The mother that their nearly three-year-old daughter wouldn't even remember, except in pictures from the past. He carried one of them, their engagement photo, in his wallet. Not their official one, but one of the outtakes where they were both laughing so hard at one of their inside jokes. They'd been friends so long that they'd had many of them. When Ann died, Clark hadn't lost just his wife; he'd lost his best friend.

He blinked to clear his vision and peer harder through the windshield of the state police SUV. This far out in the country, the street signs were hard to find through all the overhanging branches and weeds growing up alongside the rural Michigan roads. But as he studied the area, he noticed a sign dangling from a bent post. On it was the name of the street he was trying to find.

He released a shaky sigh as he turned onto the gravel road, past the mailboxes all bunched at the end of it. From the number of boxes, it was fair to conclude that there were five properties along the private drive, all set back from the road too far for him to see beyond the trees to the home.

There were a lot of areas like this in Coral County, places where old mobile homes that had originally been used as vacation properties were now inhabited year-round, despite not having enough insulation to hold up to the brutal Michigan winters. At least winter was a couple of months away yet, but the CPS investigator hadn't requested law enforcement to accompany her while she evaluated a child's living conditions.

According to the dispatcher, someone had called Miss Potter to request her help, had begged the CPS investigator to save the caller's child. An ambulance had also been notified, but there weren't many in the area, so it was definitely going to take longer to arrive. Hopefully, nobody needed more medical attention than his first-aid skills and kit could provide.

Clark wasn't sure what the situation was. The dispatcher had said that Miss Potter only had her caller's word that she was in danger. No proof. Maybe the call had just been a prank. Or something else…

A reason to lure her out here. There had been speculation that was the case with the domestic violence call that had claimed Ann's life. That the caller had just wanted to lure the cops to their death since nobody else had been found at the scene.

This area would be the perfect place for an ambush.

It was so desolate he couldn't even identify which driveways went with which properties, because there were no numbers, either on the trees or the posts near the road. Hoping his GPS was right, he followed its direction and turned into a driveway that was more dirt and deep ruts than gravel. What appeared to be fresh tires marks wound down it. He followed them to a sedan that was so covered with dust and dirt that it was hard to determine if it was black or gray or even navy blue. It was parked near a rusted-out metal mobile home. He must have found the right address, because beneath the layer of dust on the vehicle was a State Department logo on the door, and the equally dust-covered license plate was also State Department, so the CPS investigator had probably driven it here.

Clark peered through his windshield and through the sedan's dust-covered windows. The vehicle was empty. Where was she?

Dispatch had advised her to wait for him. CPS workers went through training, so she had to know that was the protocol in situations like this. Where there was the possibility of danger, she had to wait for law enforcement to arrive first at the scene. Even when the police arrived first, like Ann had, it was sometimes still dangerous for everyone, including law enforcement.

Why hadn't Miss Potter waited for him? Didn't she know she could be risking her life? Maybe she hadn't been on the job long enough to have had a close call, to know how dangerous a profession it could be.

He touched the radio on the collar of his dark-blue uniform shirt, reported that he'd arrived at what appeared to be the correct address and then pushed open the door. Just as he slid from beneath the steering wheel, a scream rang out, shattering the eerie silence of the rural countryside.

Since the dust-covered sedan was the only one here, that scream might be from the CPS investigator. Maybe she was alone. Or maybe she wasn't alone, and she'd screamed because someone was hurting her. Clark unclipped his holster and withdrew his weapon as he started toward the rickety steps leading up to the door of the rusted mobile home.

He hoped he wasn't too late…just as Ann's backup had been too late to protect her, to save her.

He hoped he wasn't too late to protect and save Miss Potter.

TWO

Renae's throat burned from the scream that shock had rent out of her the minute she'd pushed open the door and stumbled across the horrific scene inside the trailer. The body was lying just inside the door on the kitchen floor, with beer cans and cigarette butts strewn around it and blood pooled beneath it.

Beneath *her*. Long blond hair was tangled around her pale face, and her green eyes, open but slightly glazed, were fixed in a blank stare.

Ella...

Renae hadn't made it in time to help her. Ella had warned her on the phone that it was too late for her. The young woman gripped a cell phone in her hand, the screen black and shattered. Someone had destroyed it just as they'd destroyed the young mother. Her clothes were torn and bloody, her arms and hands covered in blood and deep gouges, but as hard as she must have fought off her attacker, she hadn't been able to avoid the knife. She'd apparently been stabbed more than once.

A gasp slipped through Renae's lips, and tears

flooded her eyes, blurring the horrible image before her. *Poor, Ella...*

Please, God, protect and comfort her in Your loving arms.

He would take care of Ella now, unlike Renae, who'd failed her. And the baby...

Where was the baby?

The only sound in the home had been Renae's scream. No baby's cry had echoed it. She hadn't heard him earlier, either, when Ella had called her. There had been no noise in the background then. The killer must have...

Killed him, too?

Or taken him?

Renae was afraid to look for the baby now even though concern for Simon was what had compelled her to break protocol and go into the mobile home before the state police sergeant arrived. With no other cars parked in the driveway, not even Ella's, she'd figured that nobody was home, except maybe for the baby.

And the thought of him being left alone...

It had compelled her to rush inside...to this horrific scene.

Behind her something creaked, and the floor seemed to shift and sag. She was no longer alone. She whirled around to stare down the barrel of a gun. This time, she didn't scream. She wasn't horrified or afraid.

Law enforcement had arrived. And while he didn't look happy and had a deep scowl on his handsome face, he wasn't going to shoot her. His appearance was as shocking as how suddenly he'd arrived. His features were so chiseled, his blue eyes so intense as he stared at her. She was pretty tall herself, but he was even taller.

"Miss Potter?" he asked, his voice so deep it seemed to rumble out of his chest.

She nodded.

"You were supposed to stay away until I arrived and secured the scene. Rushing in here like you did, without protection, could have gotten you killed!" he exclaimed, his voice cracking now with emotion.

She didn't want to think about that, didn't want to think about herself at all right now. Just Ella. And the baby.

"You were late," she said.

He shook his head. "I was actually earlier than I thought I would be. And apparently so were you." He stepped around her, as if blocking her from whatever threat might be inside, and his attention focused on the woman lying on the floor.

From the way Ella's eyes were open and unblinking, it was clear that she was already dead. At least it had been clear to Renae.

The officer knelt beside the body and slid his fingers around the woman's wrist to check for a pulse. His breath slipped out between his teeth in something that was more like a hiss than a sigh, and after his breath, something else slipped out of his mouth—something like a prayer.

But all Renae could hear was *"God, have mercy..."*

Hopefully, He had had mercy on the young mother and she had not suffered too much before she died. But she shouldn't have died so young, so violently, and left a child behind on his own.

Tears stung Renae's eyes, but she blinked them back.

"You shouldn't have come inside," the state police sergeant said as he peered at her over his broad shoulder. "We need to keep the scene secure, protect the evid—"

Interrupting him again, she said, "I need to protect a child. That's why I came inside. I was worried that the baby was here alone. Ella Sedlecky has a child. His name is Simon, and he's not even three months old."

The officer sucked in a breath and rose up from his crouch to look around the place. "Where is he?" That deep rumble held a world of dread now, just like what was coiled in the pit of Renae's stomach.

She shook her head. "I don't know. The last thing Ella said on the phone was for me to save her baby. She must have known it was too late for her." Had she already been stabbed when she called? Emotion rushed up on Renae, choking her as sobs formed in the back of her throat.

"The phone is in her hand," the officer observed. "But broken. Her killer might have still been here when she made that call."

Renae shivered at the thought that the killer had been listening while Ella pleaded with her to help. That person could have helped her instead of just watching her die.

What kind of monster did that? What kind of monster could kill a woman as sweet and young as Ella Sedlecky? She'd had her whole life ahead of her, just like…

Like her child.

"We have to find the baby," Renae implored the officer just as the single mother had implored her to save the child. She started through the kitchen area, where Ella was lying on the floor near the table, but before she'd taken more than a couple of steps, the officer touched her arm, then wrapped his big hand around her wrist to stop her.

"You need to go outside, Miss Potter," he told her. "I will search the home."

She tugged her wrist away. "But the baby could be hurt—"

"I will find him," he said, his deep voice almost vibrating with the vow. It wasn't exactly a promise, though— more like grim determination.

Was he worried, like she was, that he would find the baby the same way they'd found Ella? Dead?

"You need to step outside, Miss Potter," he said.

"What if the killer is out there?" she asked. With a hand that was shaking, she directed his attention back to Ella's battered body lying on the floor. But she quickly looked away from the young woman and back at the sergeant.

A muscle twitched along his tightly clenched jaw. "I surveyed the immediate area and didn't see any sign of anyone else around here but you. Your vehicle is the only one anywhere in the area," he said. "You'll be safe out there. Probably safer than in here, since I haven't had the chance to secure the scene." He gave her a pointed look with a slight narrowing of his blue eyes, like he was exasperated with her.

She was exasperated with him. "If there's no vehicle

out there but mine and yours, then there's nobody in here, either." Except maybe for Simon.

"It's a crime scene," he reiterated, and he pointed at the door. His hand was steady, though. As steady as he seemed despite what they'd found.

She was shaken, and not just over Ella, but Simon, too. Where was he?

"Look for the baby," she said before she pushed open the door and stepped onto the first of the wooden steps. The sole of her shoe slipped on the weathered wood, and she had to reach out and grasp the railing before she fell. As she steadied herself, she noticed a bright speck of blue in the overgrown bushes beside those stairs. Blue yarn, knitted together to form a baby's bootie, but the blue yarn was stained with blood.

Another scream climbed up the back of her throat, rising from her heart, which was filled with fear for that poor baby. But instead of releasing the cry, she prayed.

Please, God, please make sure that Simon is unharmed, that he's safe.

But could he be safe if he was with whoever had done that to Ella? Because who else could have taken him away from the scene but the last person who'd been there, the person who had killed his mother?

The minute the door closed behind the distraught CPS worker, Clark reached for the radio on his collar and reported what he'd found at the scene. What she had found first. No wonder she'd screamed.

This was probably the first murder victim Miss Potter had ever stumbled across. The CPS investigator looked quite young, so she might not have been at her job that long. Along with her youth, he'd also noticed that she was pretty, with long, curly brown hair and big, dark eyes. He really shouldn't have paid her that much attention…not with everything else going on. When he'd heard her scream, he'd been so afraid of how he would find her, that she might have been hurt. So many fears and feelings had rushed over him, reminding him of how he'd lost Ann. He hadn't been there because, after having Sierra, they'd worked different shifts so one of them would always be with her. But he'd read the report. He knew how it had happened. How everyone had been too late to help Ann.

Just as he and the CPS worker had been too late to help this young woman. As he spoke into his radio, he continued to inspect the interior of the mobile home. There were just two bedrooms and a bath off the hall from the small living room. Both rooms were unoccupied, as was the bathroom, and all of them were clean in comparison to the living room and kitchen. The double bed was neatly made up with throw pillows and a crisply folded quilt. The baby's room was spotless with brightly painted walls and toys and a shiny, new-looking crib. He might not have ever used that bed, though, since there was a bassinet beside the double bed. The bathroom, while worn with dated furnishings, was also clean.

So what had happened in the kitchen and living room?

It wasn't just the young woman's body and blood spilled on the floor, but food and cigarette butts and beer cans. More beer cans were scattered around the living room along with some drug paraphernalia.

The condition of the home was so strange with the public areas trashed and the private areas neat and tidy. Usually people threw their clutter and junk into the private areas and kept the public areas neater. Maybe she'd just had a party, one that had gotten seriously out of hand. It was still early in the afternoon, so maybe the party had happened the night before. The woman had been alive when she'd called Miss Potter just over a half hour ago, according to what the dispatcher had told him.

He crouched down near the body again. He'd already checked for a pulse to confirm that she was gone. Now he checked for any other clues that might tell him where her baby was. The cell phone was smashed, but hopefully the techs would be able to get the records of her calls and texts from it.

But the phone wasn't the only thing she held. A bit of blue material peeked out between the fingers of her other hand, the one folded beneath her. Something like yarn…like all the blankets his mother knitted and crocheted. But this wasn't a blanket. It was just a scrap of fabric. A pang struck his heart as he realized what it was.

A baby bootie.

His mother had made those, too, but hers had been pink and purple for his baby girl. For Sierra.

At nearly three years old, Sierra was too big for booties, so now Grandma made them for her dolls. His little girl, with her big blue eyes and pale-blond curls, looked like some of those dolls. Clark couldn't imagine not knowing where she was, if she was all right, and being helpless to keep her safe.

Like this poor mother…

She must have died trying to protect her baby. Maybe the killer had stabbed her first in the kitchen and re-trieved the baby from the bassinet, but the young mother, although dying, had fought to hang on to her baby. Maybe the bootie was all she'd managed to clutch as the child had been wrested away from her. To where? Where had her baby been taken?

He opened the door to the outside, and saw the CPS worker standing at the bottom of the wooden stairs. Blood smeared one of the steps; she must have had some on the bottoms of her shoes, must have stepped in the victim's blood.

He probably had, too. There was so much of it.

"Did you find him?" Miss Potter asked, her brown eyes staring intently at him. There was no hope in them, though. Either her job had already made her jaded, or she knew. Then he noticed that in one of her hands, she clutched the same thing the murder victim had: one of those blue baby booties.

THREE

Renae held her breath, and it burned in her lungs, while she waited for the sergeant to answer her question. He just stared down at her from the top of the steps near the door to the rusted mobile home. Then, finally, he slowly shook his head in reply to her question. She forced herself to breathe again, for some of the tension inside her to subside. Sergeant Mayweather not finding the baby inside was a good thing. That meant that he hadn't been killed, like his mother. Or, at the least, it meant he hadn't been killed *here*.

Panic shooting through her again, Renae said, "We have to find him. We have to find Simon." Before it was too late for him, like it was already too late for his mother. She turned to head toward her car.

But the sergeant moved quickly and caught her arm again like he had inside the home. "You're not going anywhere. We have to wait until the techs get here, until the scene is secure, and until whichever detective is going to investigate the murder has a chance to question you. I called, but the techs are at least a half hour away."

A siren whined in the distance, though. It must be the ambulance. The one that Ella didn't need now.

Renae tugged on her arm, easily pulling it free of his loose grasp. "That baby is only three months old," she reminded him. "If he's out there alone somewhere, he's totally vulnerable."

The sergeant reached out again but only pointed at what she clutched in her hand. "You're holding a bootie. Where did you find it?"

She stared down at the bit of blue yarn, surprised to find it in her grip. She'd seen it and… She shuddered. "It was stuck in the bushes next to the stairs," she admitted. She knew it was evidence and she shouldn't have touched it. She didn't even remember touching it, but…

She drew in a deep breath. She was better than this. She'd worked some bad cases before. Had been too late to save some children…

So why wasn't she handling this better?

God, give me the strength…the courage…the wisdom…

She knew those weren't all the correct words or order of the prayer, not according to how it had been written, but it was the correct order for her of the things she needed in this moment. She needed strength first. The strength to pull herself together.

"You must be pretty new," Sergeant Mayweather said, his voice such a low, deep rumble that he might not have meant for her to hear it. "I'm sure this is difficult for you, especially if you were the one who was working with that girl—"

"What are you implying?" she interjected. "That this

is my fault?" She wasn't necessarily denying that it was, but something about his tone put her on the defensive, made her feel threatened somehow, even though he was no longer pointing his gun at her like he had when he'd stepped inside the mobile home. In that moment, she hadn't been afraid, but now…

Now she was afraid that whatever he was implying was probably right. Somehow she'd missed something. No. She'd missed *someone*: a killer.

The sergeant replied, "I might not have all the information correct from Dispatch, but I was told this girl called you for help. And you knew where she lived, so you've crossed paths with her before. Why?"

"Someone called in an anonymous complaint about her to CPS over a month ago. They claimed that she was partying and neglecting her child. I found no evidence of that."

He arched an eyebrow. "Really? No evidence of the partying? The kitchen and living room are full of beer cans and—"

"It wasn't like that when I came to inspect the living conditions," she interrupted to defend herself, but mostly to defend Ella.

He shrugged. "I imagine that people make sure to clean up when they know you're coming."

"She didn't know I was coming," Renae insisted. "And even the ones who do know aren't able to get their home as clean as this place was then. There was no dust on the blinds, no cobwebs in the corners. It was cleaner than my apartment is." That was probably because she was rarely home long enough to do more than sleep, and when she was, the last thing she wanted to do was housework. Maybe she should accept Mom's offer to hire the cleaning service she'd suggested the last time she had come to visit.

"The bedrooms and bathroom were like that," the sergeant acknowledged, and his brow furrowed slightly. "And if she'd had a party, the bathroom probably wouldn't have been so neat and clean. Partygoers wouldn't have cleaned up after themselves like that."

"What are you thinking?" she asked. "That someone staged the kitchen to look like there'd been a party, like her murder was premeditated?" In her experience, when a life was taken, it was in a moment of rage or passion. The death was more the consequence of a horrible impulse or total lack of control rather than of a carefully thought-out plan. Her skin suddenly chilled, and she shivered.

"You can wait in your car if you're getting cold," the sergeant suggested. He must have noticed her reaction and misconstrued it to the weather.

While the afternoon was slipping away, and the sun was behind overcast clouds, it wasn't the temperature that had chilled Renae. It was the thought that someone could be so evil as to have plotted to kill a young woman as dedicated to her child as Ella Sedlecky had been. So dedicated that her last request had been for him and not herself.

Renae shook her head. "I can't wait. I need to find that baby. He's in danger." She held out the bootie spattered with blood. His mother's blood? Or his? "This proves it. It must have fallen off him when the killer took him."

The sergeant drew in a deep breath before releasing it in a ragged sigh. "There is one in his mother's hand, too."

Renae gasped. "You mean…she fought over her baby…"

She could imagine Ella using the last bit of her strength to try to save her child while the killer pulled him away from her. Tears stung Renae's eyes as emotion overwhelmed her. But why hadn't Renae heard his cries? Had Ella called her after the killer took off with the baby? Was that why she'd wanted Renae to protect him from the person who'd killed his mother, the person who'd taken him?

"I have to find him. Now." She wasn't going to wait to start her search, and if the sergeant wanted to stop her, he was going to have to arrest her.

If other units hadn't pulled into the driveway behind the ambulance, lights flashing and sirens blaring, Clark might have had to physically detain Miss Potter to stop her from rushing off to search for the missing baby. He understood her urgency; it burned inside him, too, quickening his pulse. He couldn't imagine not having any idea where Sierra was. If she was safe…

If she was hurt…

The bloodstained booties that the crime scene unit had collected suggested the baby had probably been here during the murder. At three months, he hadn't gotten away from the home on his own. Someone must have taken him, and that someone was probably the same person who'd taken his mother from him.

Her killer.

Two morticians from the county coroner's office carried the gurney that held Ella's body zipped into a black bag down the steps from the mobile home. They passed Miss Potter, who shuddered. Clark barely resisted the urge to shudder himself. He'd seen dead bodies before, but it never failed to affect him. He closed his eyes for a moment and offered up a silent prayer, taking comfort in his faith that the young woman was now with God. And with Ann. His fierce wife would help Him protect Ella Sedlecky.

He had to help protect the young woman's child, or at least locate him. While a couple of other units had responded to his call, as sergeant, he was still the highest-ranking officer at the scene. The other two units were another state trooper, who only had traffic experience, and a Coral County sheriff's deputy in a county that was already stretched thin. Clark knew that because he lived in Coral, where most of the population was below the poverty level, like Ella Sedlecky.

"So what are you going to do to find the baby?" Miss Potter asked him. Clearly, she'd figured out what he had.

This was going to be his investigation. "Let me make a call..." he murmured. He had to actually make two. One to his captain and another to his aunt, who was currently watching his daughter.

"I don't have time," Miss Potter said and shook her head, making her long, dark curls tumble around her shoulders. "No, Simon doesn't have time."

"Do you have any idea where to look for him?" Clark asked.

She froze for a moment, as if just realizing that she had no idea. "I'll go through my notes from the case. My interviews…" She headed toward her car then. While the coroner's van drove away, the crime tech unit van, which had arrived right after the ambulance Clark had turned away, still blocked the narrow drive, so he wasn't worried about her driving off without him. Yet…

He stood near her vehicle to pull out his cell and make his calls. The captain confirmed what he'd already deduced for himself.

"There's no one else we can pull right now," Captain Monica Chapin told him.

"But I'm needed at the training center," he reminded her. And he was needed at home the most. "I'll help find the baby." His conscience wouldn't give him any peace until he did. "But I shouldn't be investigating a murder. That's beyond my expertise."

"You've conducted the preliminary interviews for the detective unit before," she reminded him. "You can do this. Take good notes, and when a detective is available, he or she will take over the case."

"But…" He had Sierra and his mother to think about, to worry about, but right now, finding that missing baby was the priority. His daughter and his mother would agree. Sierra loved "bee-bees" and always made a fuss whenever they saw a baby at church or the playground or the grocery store. Sierra went everywhere with him. Even to work. Her picture was inside his shirt pocket, next to his heart.

He drew in a deep breath. "Okay, Captain. I'll keep you updated."

"I know," she said.

Even though he wanted to check on Sierra, he dreaded making his next call. His mom and Sierra would understand his need to find the missing baby, but he didn't think his aunt would be as understanding if he was late coming home. The former elementary school teacher didn't have much patience for kids since her retirement a few years ago. "Clark, I thought this was just going to be for an hour or so."

"I'm sorry, Aunt Kelly, but I have no one else—"

"Your stepdad—"

"Needs to stay with Mom," he said. "She's having surgery, getting screws and pins in her ankle to hold it in place." She'd fallen and broken it while babysitting Sierra. He would never forget how frightened they'd both sounded when she'd called him. He wished he could have stayed with his mom and with Sierra.

"I can switch places with him," Aunt Kelly offered. "I can stay with my sister, and Bradford can watch Sierra." She sounded almost desperate now to get out of babysitting duty. She couldn't hate kids, not after all the years she'd taught. She'd even once been licensed as a foster parent to help out with a student whose family had been deported.

"Is she being that difficult?" he asked with concern. Usually Sierra was so very sweet and well-behaved.

"She's been crying a lot," she said. "And I've lost my touch, Clark. I don't know how to make her feel better."

A twinge of concern struck his heart. "I'm sorry. Let me talk to her, please." As he heard his aunt pass the phone to his daughter, he switched his call to speaker.

"Daddy…" The soft voice quavered out of his cell.

"Yes, sweetheart. Are you all right?" he asked.

"Uh-huh, Grammy got hurt."

"I know, sweetheart, but she's going to be fine," he assured his little girl. Of course, her tears were for someone else. That was how sweet and sensitive she was. "The doctors are fixing Grammy's ankle right now."

"I cou'n't fix her."

"I know, honey, but you did really well," he praised her. "You brought Grammy her phone. You were so very brave. Now I need to ask you to be brave for just a little while longer, okay?"

"'Kay, Daddy."

"I can't leave work to come home until later today," he said. With how quickly the afternoon was slipping away behind dark clouds, it might be night before he managed to clock out. "So I need you to be really good for Aunt Kelly. Okay?"

"'Kay, Daddy." Her breath shuddered out of his phone in a ragged little sigh that had a pang striking his heart so hard again that he rubbed his chest. "Whatcha doing at work?" she asked.

He paused a moment, considering if he should tell her anything or lie. She was still a few months shy of three years old, a baby in some ways, but she was also an old soul in other ways. With her empathy and her spirituality. "I'm looking for a baby," he said.

"A bee-bee?" she queried and now her voice quavered with excitement. "Is the bee-bee 'kay?"

Clark kept internally praying that he was, but he had no idea. However, he didn't want her worrying any more than she already was, and he regretted that he'd mentioned Simon. "I'm sure he is, sweetheart. His mom just isn't able to tell us where he is right now, so I'm helping another lady look for him."

"What lady?"

"Miss Potter," he said. "She helps kids."

"Is she nice?" she asked.

He really had no idea. She'd been upset, rightfully, since he'd arrived at the scene. And then she'd also been defensive with him and impatient. Probably justifiably so with the impatience as well.

"I'm sure she is," he replied. Otherwise she wouldn't have chosen the profession she had. And she wouldn't care as much as she obviously cared. "Now I better go help her." He glanced up then to find Miss Potter standing in front of him. She didn't look impatient now. Her brow was furrowed as she stared up at him. "Sierra, remember to be my brave little girl."

"'Kay, Daddy," Sierra's voice said from the cell. "And bring the bee-bee here when you find 'im."

His lips involuntarily curved into a slight smile. She really wanted a little baby brother or sister so badly. "I can't do that, sweetheart," he said. He glanced at the trailer then and reminded himself that he couldn't bring the child back to his own home, either. Not now that it was a crime scene and his mother was dead.

But it wasn't his job to determine where to place the child; that was Miss Potter's task. His job was to find the baby and find the baby's mother's killer.

In that order...

* * *

Peering through the branches at the vehicles parked in the driveway had the killer's heart thumping hard and fast with fear. Crime scene unit. Had they found anything? Had any evidence been left behind…besides what they had staged?

The beer cans.

The drug paraphernalia.

While not everything had gone according to plan, at least there had been time to get those from the vehicle, to spread them around the kitchen and living room before anybody had responded to Ella's call for help. Going back into the trailer had been a good thing— finding Ella on her cell…with that card in front of her, the card for the Child Protective Services investigator, Renae Potter, with her number…

It was smeared with blood now—Ella's blood—and crumpled in the killer's pocket. But the blood was really on Renae Potter's hands. Surely those things in the kitchen and the living room would show the CPS investigator how wrong she had been to not remove the child from that place, from that stupid girl.

Ella was dead now, though. She couldn't fool anyone else into thinking that she actually deserved to keep her baby. The baby was gone now and would never be returned to Ella Sedlecky.

FOUR

Renae parked her state vehicle in the nearly empty lot of the county health department building. Cornfields surrounded the sprawling old brick building that had once been a school. Renae was one of the few staff that worked out of the building, since CPS workers were hard to hire and even harder to retain in this area. Knowing how badly she was needed here had been one of the reasons why Renae had left the city— for this position.

Her mother had been another.

The only time the lot was ever full was when the health department offered free vaccinations. Another vehicle pulled in next to hers—Sergeant Mayweather's state police SUV. She jumped out of the driver's seat, gathered up her laptop and phones, and slammed the door shut. Before she could reach for the passenger's side door of his SUV, Sergeant Mayweather was there, opening the door for her. For a big man, he moved fast, but then that was probably a requirement of his job in law enforcement—speed. He'd certainly kept up with her driving. He had to understand her urgency. She'd wanted to drive herself to track down all of the people she'd interviewed when she'd investigated that complaint against Ella, but he'd insisted that it wasn't safe. One of them could be her killer.

Renae prayed that wasn't the case, that she hadn't missed an opportunity to have prevented the young woman's murder.

"It's not your fault, Miss Potter," Mayweather said, as if he'd read her mind, or maybe he'd just realized how heavily guilt was weighing on it.

Her shoulders sagged with the heavy burden of it and her laptop bag. She swung the bag inside his vehicle before settling onto the seat. Instead of closing the door for her, he leaned down, stared intently at her and repeated, "It's not your fault."

Ignoring the little rush of awareness that shot through her due to his closeness and his chiseled jaw and his vivid blue eyes, she remembered how hurt and defensive she'd been over how he'd reacted earlier. "That's not the impression you gave me back at the scene," she pointed out. "You seemed to think I hadn't done my job when I chose to close Ella's case without removing Simon from her custody."

"I'm sorry I gave you that impression," he said. "I really don't have enough information to judge. It was just the condition of the home..."

"Being poor doesn't mean that a parent can't take care of their child," she said, which was something she'd had to point out in the past to her own mother.

"I was talking about the cigarette butts and other stuff."

"Ella took and passed a drug test," Renae said. "I really don't believe that stuff was hers."

Instead of arguing with her, Sergeant Mayweather nodded. "I'm beginning to believe that, too. When the body was moved, the crime scene tech told me nothing was under it."

"Like the stuff had been dumped around her after…" She could have shuddered at the thought, but instead of being scared, she was indignant for Ella. "She wasn't into parties."

But whoever had killed her had wanted it to look like she was, just like the person who'd filed the complaint. They had to be the same, but why?

She'd already showed the sergeant the transcript of the anonymous call. She didn't want to mention it again because it brought up all the guilt she felt over not digging deeper into that. Instead, she shared her impression of the young mother. "Ella worked hard to support her son and herself on her own." Which she wouldn't have had to do if she would have forced her ex-husband to take a paternity test and own up to his responsibilities. But maybe there was a reason she hadn't wanted him involved in her life.

"Where did she work?" Sergeant Mayweather asked. "And would she have been there today?"

"It was where she was every day," Renae replied. "At the Coral Creek Bar and Grill. And while she's there, another waitress, Lauren, watches Simon for her. Since Lauren's husband is deployed, Lauren is essentially a single parent, too. When Ella's shift ends, she watches Lauren's daughter and Simon."

The sergeant's tall body tensed. "Could there have been two children at her place?"

She shook her head. "No. She stays—stayed—at Lauren's apartment in town and watched them both there. Lauren doesn't have a car and wouldn't be able to pick up…" She couldn't remember her daughter's name, but Renae had it in her notes somewhere. And it was also in the file that had been opened and closed on Lauren six months ago. Renae hadn't investigated that case; her boss had handled it before Renae had started with Coral County. Lauren had known who'd called on her, though—her disapproving mother-in-law, who was, unfortunately, also one of the owners of the restaurant where she and Ella worked.

Mayweather's tension eased slightly. "Is it possible that Ella didn't have either child?"

"I can't imagine her coming home without him," Renae said. "But she should be watching both kids at Lauren's right now. Maybe the restaurant closed for the day…" It was happening in other places, even in the city, according to Renae's mother, because of staffing shortages.

He shrugged. "I don't know, but until the techs have a chance to retrieve all the data from her phone, we can't use it to retrace her steps. We can only go off what you know about her, Miss Potter."

Renae had thought she'd known enough to conclude that Ella would never endanger her child. But Simon was clearly in danger now. That wasn't Ella's fault; it might be Renae's if she'd missed something—

something that could have forewarned her about what could happen to the baby's mother.

He stepped back as if he was going to swing her door shut, but before he could, she said, "Renae. Call me Renae."

He nodded, closed her door and walked around to the driver's side. "So, Renae, let's start at the Coral Creek Bar and Grill," he said as he slid behind the steering wheel. "We can see if it's open, and if it is, we can talk to her bosses and coworkers, including Lauren, if she's there, and see what we can learn from them."

She nodded now, surprised he remembered that she'd told him Ella worked for a couple who owned the restaurant. After he'd hung up from the call with his daughter, she'd read the highlights of her report to him. But she'd been distracted since she'd overheard his call with his young daughter, and how upset and yet sweet she seemed. At the time, Renae had felt guilty for eavesdropping on his private conversation, so she hadn't asked any personal questions, had focused on the professional exchange only. On Ella and Simon. In addition to what she'd read to him, she had also showed the sergeant the final report, as well as all the notes she'd taken while investigating the anonymous complaint against Ella.

But as he drove toward the small village of Coral Creek, she couldn't control her curiosity any longer. "How old is your daughter?" she asked.

His lips curved into a slight smile. "Two and three quarters," he said. "And she will certainly remind you of those three quarters because she's not a *bee-bee* anymore." His smile widened; he obviously adored his child.

"She seems to like babies," Renae said. She was still surprised that he'd shared with his little girl why he was going to be late getting home from work. Even before he'd said how old his daughter was, Renae had suspected she was too young to hear anything about his job.

His smile slipped away, and he sighed. "She's obsessed with babies."

She glanced at his hands gripping the steering wheel. He didn't wear a wedding band, but then a lot of married people were forgoing rings nowadays. She might have chosen to do that herself, but she'd decided long ago that it was smarter to forgo marriage entirely. Which was another reason why she'd had to move away from her mother...

"Good to know my mom's not the only one," she muttered.

Her mother wanted grandchildren. She didn't understand that Renae was helping far more children by never having any of her own. The CPS workers with kids, with spouses, couldn't work the hours the job sometimes required. They weren't willing to go out on nights and weekends, when the clock started ticking on finding a child.

Like the clock was ticking on the search for Simon...

Sergeant Mayweather glanced over at her now, at her hands, like she'd glanced at his. She didn't wear any rings, either—no jewelry of any kind. She used her phone to keep track of the time, setting alarms on it to let her know how long she had left to make contact, to do her interviews, to fill out the report and submit it to her supervisor. After she'd called 911, she'd called her supervisor and told her what was going on while she'd driven to Ella's. Like the dispatcher, Glenda had reminded her to wait for the police, to let them handle the situation. It had been too late for anyone to handle it, though.

"I'm not married," she told him. "Something else that bugs my mom." Heat rushed to her face with embarrassment because she'd admitted such a thing to him. "I'm sorry for the overshare. You obviously don't care about my marital status. Probably the only one who actually does is my mother."

He chuckled. "No need to apologize. I overshared to my daughter." His mouth slid from a smile to a frown at the admission. "I had to check in on her, though, while my aunt's watching her."

"Your mother was hurt?" she asked. She'd overheard his entire conversation but was embarrassed to admit that as well.

He nodded. "She was standing on a chair to water some hanging plants and slipped and fell onto the cement patio. She landed badly on her ankle and broke it." He flinched as if his mother's pain physically affected him.

"That's terrible. I'm so sorry." She offered up a silent prayer for the woman, for her to heal quickly and fully.

"My daughter was the only one with her at the time," he said. "That's why Sierra was so upset. She must have been terrified…" He trailed off and cleared his throat. "Sorry, I know that situation was nothing like today…"

"When Ella called me for help," Renae said, finishing for him and then admitted, "That was horrifying." She drew in a shaky breath. "But I'm not two and three quarters years old. Your daughter had to be incredibly shaken up. You couldn't stay with her?"

He shook his head. "I clocked out for a bit until my stepdad got to the hospital so he could stay with Mom and until my aunt could come and pick up my daughter."

"What about your wife?" she asked, her curiosity overwhelming her now. Maybe they were divorced. "I mean, Sierra's mother?"

"My wife, Sierra's mother, died two years ago," he replied, his deep voice flat and matter-of-fact, but the way his shoulders drooped and his jaw tightened indicated that he wasn't over it. He still missed her, probably always would.

"I'm sorry…" She couldn't imagine loving anyone enough to marry them, let alone loving and losing that person.

"Ann was also a state trooper," he said. "She died after responding to a domestic violence call. She was shot just as she stepped out of her vehicle. Didn't even have a chance…"

She gasped at the horror of the woman's death, and her heart ached for the loss the sergeant and his daughter had suffered.

His face flushed. "I'm sorry, I just overshared with you now, but I wanted you to understand why I reacted like I did at you walking into that mobile home before the scene was secured."

Because she could have been shot, like his wife was.

A shiver raced down her spine as she realized how much danger she had put herself in. She knew better than that. But she'd been so worried about Simon and Ella. She wouldn't have been able to help them, or anyone else, if she'd gotten herself killed, though.

"I'm sorry," he said again.

She wasn't sure what he was apologizing for—how he'd treated her at the scene or telling her why he'd treated her the way he had?

Before she could ask, he continued, "You didn't ask for the details of Ann's death, but people usually do..."

Because they were nosy, like she'd been. "I probably would have asked," she admitted. "I've gotten so used to interviewing people, and that involves asking some real personal questions."

"How long have you been with CPS?" He glanced across the console at her again, as if trying to gauge her age.

Due to her youthful appearance, people usually misjudged by a few years, thinking she'd just graduated college. "Seven years."

"In Coral County?"

She shook her head. "No. River City area."

He pursed his lips and let out a soft whistle. "You must have been a lot busier there."

The city on the west side of the state was even bigger than Detroit. So she understood why he might think that, but she corrected his misconception. "No. River City had a lot more investigators on staff than Coral does. I'm much busier here than I ever was back in the city."

"How long have you been here?"

"Just for a few months," she said. Long enough to understand why investigators didn't last, why they usually transferred to bigger cities or quit the job entirely. In order to investigate every case within the time constraints, a person had to work just about around the clock every day, including weekends.

"That must be why I haven't met you," he said. "That, and after my wife died, I took a position as a training officer."

Because he didn't want to leave his daughter an orphan. He didn't say it, but she suspected that was his reason. The sudden urge to reach out to him, to touch his hand or his shoulder in a show of sympathy, nearly overwhelmed her, but she resisted the impulse. She had to keep this professional…for so many reasons. The most important one being Simon.

Where was the baby?

"There's the restaurant," she said, pointing through the windshield at the steel-sided pole building that had been converted to a bar and grill. Despite its simple decor, the place was usually packed since it was one of the few restaurants to eat in the area. Renae had stopped in a few times for a meal between interviews. It had Wi-Fi, so she'd been able to work on her reports on her laptop. "If Ella wasn't home with Simon, she was working here."

That was what everyone had told her—that the young mother took no time for herself and certainly not to party. So someone must have planted those empty beer cans and other things in her kitchen and living room area.

"This is a long way from her home," the sergeant observed. "How did she get here?"

"She has a vehicle," Renae said. She hadn't remembered what it was until she'd found the reference to it in her notes. "Like the home, she also inherited her grandfather's old truck."

Instead of stopping in the parking lot beside the building, Sergeant Mayweather drove around it, and as he turned his SUV into the alley behind, he nearly collided with the grille of a rusted old truck. He braked and stopped without striking it.

"That's it!" Renae exclaimed. The vehicle was sitting at an odd angle with one side higher than the other.

Sergeant Mayweather stopped the SUV, and they both jumped out. As Renae approached the truck, she saw why it was tilted. The tires on the driver's side had both been slashed with deep gashes in the rubber, just like...

Like Ella.

Had the same knife been used?

"This is why her vehicle wasn't at her place," Sergeant Mayweather remarked as he surveyed the damage. He touched the radio on the collar of his navy blue shirt and requested the crime scene techs to impound and process the truck for evidence. He must have considered the same thing she had; that the murder weapon might have been used first, here on Ella's truck's tires.

"So how did she get home?" Renae wondered aloud.

"Let's find out," the sergeant said as he locked up his vehicle and headed toward the door of the restaurant that opened onto the alley. They stepped inside the kitchen, where the air was heavy with the smell of hot grease from the steaming fryers and hamburgers that sizzled on the griddle.

A cook, who looked more like a fisherman, with pieces of tackle dangling from his bucket hat, glanced over at them. "You're supposed to come in the front door," he remarked. "Isn't anybody out there yet?"

The sergeant's brow furrowed at the cook's question. "What do you mean? You're here alone?"

The guy's head bobbed. "The night waitress didn't come in, and I don't know where the bosses got to. I've been running the place alone since Ella left after lunch."

"How?" the sergeant asked him.

"How?" The guy repeated the question and then shrugged. "It's not been too busy, just a couple regulars who've helped themselves at the bar and told me through the window what they wanted to eat." He pointed toward the window to the bar area. Heat lamps illuminated the stainless-steel surface, where a few stray fries and potato chips had fallen off the plates that must have been set there awaiting a waitress to pick them up. But there was no waitress now.

"I meant how did Ella leave?" Mayweather clarified. "Her truck is in the alley."

"It is?" The guy finally focused on the sergeant. "You're a cop. What are you doing here? Did something happen to the Caufmans? Is that why they're not here?"

"The Caufmans?" Mayweather repeated.

"The owners," Renae explained, saving the cook from having to reply. She'd told him that Ella worked for a couple but hadn't included their names. "Greg and Bobbi Jo Caufman own the restaurant."

The trooper nodded. "Okay." Then he focused on the frazzled cook again. "Did one of them drive Ella home?"

Renae tensed. Could one of them have hurt her?

The cook shrugged. "I don't know. Nobody told me nothing. I didn't even know I was alone until the first customer after Ella left poked his head through the window." He gestured toward it again with his spatula, and grease dripped from the end of it.

Renae's stomach churned with anxiety. "Hasn't Lauren showed up yet today?" Could something have happened to both of the young mothers?

The cook shook his head. "No. But she'd been calling out a lot, trying to stay out of Bobbi Jo's way."

That would have explained why Ella had gone home instead of staying at Lauren's to babysit her daughter and Simon. But how had she gotten home since her truck was here? And what about Simon? Could he still be at Lauren's?

"We need to go there right now," she told Mayweather and reached out to clutch the sleeve of his uniform, tugging him back toward that door to the alley.

If someone had killed Ella in order to take her son, whoever was with him now was in danger.

Clark understood Miss Potter's—Renae's—urgency. He felt it, too, and not just because of her hand gripping his arm. It was in the pit of his stomach. The nearly empty restaurant also unsettled him. It was so eerie, like the set of a horror movie where something tragic was about to happen. But that tragedy had already happened at Ella Sedlecky's home, to Ella Sedlecky.

He was worried about what they might find at the other waitress's house, if they found her at all. "I want to make sure the crime scene techs show up here to process the truck," he said. "And when they do, you should stay here with them while I check out this Lauren's place."

He didn't want her stumbling across the same scene she had just a couple of hours ago. He didn't want her finding another murder victim, or worse yet, the murderer.

"I need to see her, too," Renae insisted. "If Simon is with her, I'll have to be there to take custody of him."

Remembering those bloodstained baby booties, Clark doubted that Lauren had him. *Please, God, don't let Ella's killer have that child.*

"Please." Renae implored him the same way he was imploring God to help.

He only wished he had enough power to grant her wish, which he was pretty sure was the same as his. To find the baby alive and safe.

"I have to find him," Renae said. "It's my job."

He suspected it was more than a job to her for some reason, or she wouldn't be so willing to put herself in danger. She wasn't worried about herself, but she was worried about a defenseless baby. Clark not only understood that, but also respected her dedication to the child.

He released a shaky breath and nodded. "Okay."

"What's going on? Why are the police here?" a man

asked as he shoved open the back door so hard that it slapped against the wall behind it. The guy was taller than Clark, and while older than him, he was muscular, with big arms and a barrel chest. He started toward the cook until he saw Clark and Renae and abruptly stopped. Then he held out his hand toward Clark. "Officer, I'm the owner. Greg Caufman. Is there a problem?"

Clark held out his hand to shake. Caufman clasped his hand hard and shook it a little too vehemently for a polite introduction. What was his deal? Was he just one of those aging guys trying to prove he was strong and vital yet?

"Didn't you see the damage to Ella Sedlecky's truck?" Clark asked the man.

"Ella called the cops about some flat tires?" Greg asked, his mouth curving into a slight, almost condescending grin.

"Slashed tires," Clark corrected him. "And, no, *she* didn't call the police."

The guy glanced at Miss Potter then, and his dark eyes widened in recognition and understanding of who had called. "You're *that* social worker," he remarked. "You came around here a few weeks ago asking about Ella and her kid."

She nodded. "Ella called me earlier today—"

"Her boss doesn't need to know about that," Clark interrupted before she could reveal the young woman's murder. He hoped by not divulging her death that Caufman might reveal more about Ella. "Did you give her a ride home today, Greg?" he asked.

The guy narrowed his eyes and slowly shook his head. "No. I think she'd already called someone…"

Earlier today, Clark had asked the crime scene unit to pull up and print out Ella's phone records for all her calls and text messages. He'd have to check to see if the report was available yet, so he could find out whom she'd called for that ride. "So you have no idea how she got home?" he said, asking the question again.

Greg shook his head again. "No. I was in my office doing the quarterly tax stuff when she told me. I offered to come out and change her tire, but she said she only had one spare. Then she walked back out. By the time I left my office, she was already gone."

The cook glanced over at his boss with a peculiar expression. His eyes squinted, and his mouth was hanging slightly open as if he was confused. As if his boss was lying…

The lawman in Clark couldn't help but wonder why the guy would lie, unless, despite Renae not revealing it, Greg Caufman somehow knew Ella was dead and that he might need an alibi.

Why would he think he needed one unless he'd been involved in her death?

Clark edged between Renae and the restaurant owner, not wanting her standing so close to a potential killer. He could protect her, unlike how he hadn't been able to protect Ella Sedlecky or Ann.

FIVE

While Renae understood that law enforcement was nearly as short-staffed as Child Protective Services was, as pretty much every industry seemed to be nowadays, she had hoped that a detective would get assigned to investigate Ella's murder. But after seeing how Sergeant Mayweather had questioned Greg Caufman, she trusted that he knew what he was doing. Hopefully that knowledge would help him find Ella's killer and, more importantly at the moment, Ella's child.

Before Sergeant Mayweather could ask Ella's boss any more questions, the restaurant owner insisted he had work to do and rushed off to his office. But the sergeant wasn't done. He turned toward the cook and asked, "Why'd you look at your boss like that? Was he lying to me?"

The cook turned his face away as it flushed a bright red, and he shook his head so hard the tackle on his hat jiggled and nearly flew off. "No, no. Of course not."

"But the way you looked at him…"

The guy shrugged. "It was nothing."

"It was something," the sergeant persisted. "Something bothered you about what he said."

The guy shrugged again. "I just thought that Bobbi Jo is the one who does all the bookkeeping. Not Greg."

The beeping noise of a commercial truck backing up drew Renae's and the cook's attention to where lights flashed through the screen door that led to the alley, but Sergeant Mayweather stayed focused on the cook.

"Where is Bobbi Jo?" he asked. "Was she here when the tires got slashed on Ella's truck?"

"I don't know. I don't know when that all happened," the guy said, his face getting even redder and his dark eyes wilder, as if he was worried that the officer was thinking he was guilty of something.

Was he? He was nearly Greg Caufman's age, probably late fifties, early sixties. He didn't look like the type who would try to go after a young single mother. But Renae had learned long ago that just because someone didn't look like the type didn't mean they weren't capable of violence, of evil.

The cook pointed his grease-dripping spatula at the back door, as if trying to send them on their way. "Did you call that tow truck?"

Sergeant Mayweather studied the guy for a long, silent moment before he turned back to Renae and gestured for her to precede him to the back door. Before she could reach for the handle, he pushed open the door, and they stepped out into the alley. The sergeant handled himself with the crime scene unit again like a pro, as if he handled murder investigations all the time. He told the techs what he was looking for, and he asked to have the records from Ella's broken phone forwarded to him ASAP.

Then he opened the passenger door of his SUV for her and hurried around to the driver's side.

"You know what you're doing," she remarked once he started his SUV and backed it out of the alley.

A slight grin curved his lips. "I'm a training officer. I wouldn't have much to teach the new hires if I didn't know what was supposed to get done."

"But you're not a detective."

"One will be taking over the case as soon as he or she is free," he said. "It's just that we're a bit understaffed and overworked right now."

"I can relate to that," she said with a heavy sigh of her own. "I have another child I need to find today."

He turned toward her. "Another one?"

"She's not in imminent danger," she assured him. "School reported that a first grader has come to class with some hygiene issues that might be because of neglect at home. She didn't go to school today and nobody answered at her house. There were no signs of physical abuse, though." So that pushed her case back on the priority list. Renae had seventy-two hours to make contact with that child. With Simon, she had twenty-four hours according to the guidelines, but she suspected the baby didn't have that long. Not twenty-four…

She wasn't even sure how long he'd been missing. How long had he been gone before Ella called her? Or had he been just ripped from her arms then? So that all she'd managed to hang on to was his baby bootie? Was that why she'd asked for Renae's help for Simon?

"There are no signs that Simon has been hurt, either," the sergeant said, as if he'd read her mind.

"The baby booties..."

"That blood probably is his mother's," he said, his deep voice even gruffer.

A little bubble of pain welled inside Renae's heart, making it ache over the cruel death of such a sweet young woman, and tears stung her eyes. Ella was with God now. It was Simon who needed Renae; Simon she might be able to help yet. She blinked away the moisture welling in her eyes and focused on giving Sergeant Mayweather directions to Lauren Caufman's place. Fortunately, it wasn't far from the Coral Creek Bar and Grill, and they arrived within minutes at the apartment, which was in an old two-story cement-block building above a take-out pizza place.

Once Mayweather parked his SUV, he turned toward her and said, "You need to stay here and wait until I make sure it's safe."

She shook her head. "No. She might not even open the door to you, but she will for me. I've talked to her before." And she needed to talk to her now, desperately.

He hesitated so long that she reached for her door handle. The passenger's door didn't lock like the back ones behind the glass partition probably did, so she wasn't trapped inside. She pushed open the door, stepped out on the worn and cracked asphalt of the old parking lot and hurried toward the back of the building.

The sergeant caught up with her quickly, but he didn't try to stop her as they clomped up the metal exterior stairwell that seemed to balance almost precariously over some kind of ventilation system with a loud, rattling fan. The metal stairs shook beneath their combined weight. When they neared the landing, the sergeant stepped around her, positioning himself between her and the door, as if he was worried she might be attacked. Or maybe he didn't want her to find what she had just a couple of hours ago: a murder victim.

Sergeant Mayweather knocked loud enough that Lauren should have heard it, but long moments passed with nobody coming to the door. He even turned the knob to check to see if it was open. Ella's door had been open when Renae arrived at her home, but this door was locked and didn't budge.

"Do you think she's gone?" he wondered aloud, glancing down at the cars in the parking lot.

"Lauren doesn't have a car," Renae reminded him. "She uses Ella's truck to get to the restaurant while Ella watches both their kids here at the apartment." They knew Ella wasn't here, and that Lauren hadn't been able to use her truck. So where was Lauren?

"I don't have a warrant to force open the door," the sergeant said. "We'll have to leave."

Renae stepped around the sergeant and knocked on it herself, her knuckles chafing against the steel door as she pounded on it with desperation gripping her. She had to find Simon. She had to… For his sake and for Ella's. Even over the rattling fan, she heard the sudden wail of a baby's cry. Simon?

Finally, the knob turned, and the door opened just a crack. Through that crack, a woman with long, stringy dark hair glared at her. "CPS. That file on me already got closed. That was just my mother-in-law causing trouble for me."

"I'm not here about that. I'm here about Simon," Renae said. "Do you have Simon?"

The woman tilted her head and repeated his name as if she didn't recognize it. "Simon?"

"Ella's baby," Renae said. "I hear him crying."

The woman opened the door farther and showed the child she held in the crook of her other arm. This baby was older than Simon with wide blue eyes and a bow headband wrapped around her little bald head.

"That's not him, I take it?" the sergeant asked.

"No. Simon has fuzzy dark hair and dark eyes."

But this baby wasn't crying, and that wail rang out again. Mayweather stepped around Renae and shouldered his way through the doorway and past the dark-haired mother holding her child.

"Where's the baby?" he asked. He didn't wait for her to answer and followed the cries through a doorway off the small living area. Seconds later, he returned with a baby cradled in his arms. He held him close to his chest as if both comforting and protecting him.

The cries subsided and the baby nearly snuggled against him. As if he knew this man would protect him...

"Oh, thank God," Renae said, relief and gratitude overwhelming her that he was alive. "That's Simon. Is he okay?"

"Of course," Lauren said. "He just cries a lot unless he's with Ella. I wasn't neglecting him or anything." She cast an accusing glance at Renae. "And neither is

Ella. She just had some trouble with her truck. That's why she's late picking him up." She glanced at the clock on the wall and sank her teeth into her bottom lip. She was worried.

And with good reason.

Renae wanted to tell her that Ella wasn't ever coming to pick up her child, but she held back that information, not wanting to interfere in the sergeant's investigation.

"So Ella called you?" Mayweather asked. "What time was that?"

She shrugged. "About one thirty. She said something happened to her truck, and she had to figure out a way to get it fixed before she could come watch the kids for me to go in to work. She said she would let Greg and Bobbi Jo know I might be a little late and she'd pay me some of her tips for me having to miss a little bit of my shift." She glanced at the clock on the stove in her small kitchenette area. "It's been more than a little bit. It's been hours."

Renae had to bite her lip now, so she wouldn't reveal why Ella hadn't shown up yet. And that she never would. She turned toward the sergeant, intent on following his lead.

Lauren focused on him, too, and her mouth fell open slightly as if she'd just realized what the reason might be for him being here. "Why are you here?" she asked him and then glanced back at Renae. "Why did you think you had to bring a cop with you? You didn't last time... when you came to talk to me about Ella." Now the color drained from her face. "Something's happened to her!"

"Why would you think that?" the sergeant asked.

"Because of you," Lauren exclaimed. "Because you wouldn't be here if everything was okay. Ella would be here." Tears pooled in her eyes now. "She's never stayed away from Simon this long before."

And Renae knew she'd been right to leave the baby with his mother a month ago. Ella had posed no threat to him. But how had Renae missed the threat to Ella? Who was it?

Clark was no closer to finding the killer, even after he questioned Ella's friend some more, but at least he'd found the baby. A baby who now had no mother.

"What about the father? Is he in the picture at all?" he asked Renae, who was riding in the back of the state police SUV. She sat next to the baby, who was safely buckled into the car seat Ella had left at Lauren's house. Lauren had said the baby had been sleeping when Ella had dropped him off, so she'd carried him inside in the car seat so she didn't wake him up.

But part of him wondered…

Had she had some indication that something might happen to her? Had she been receiving threats? He needed those records from her phone.

Renae sighed. "Ella's husband divorced her when she told him she was pregnant. He kept claiming that the baby couldn't be his and wanted nothing to do with either of them."

"Couldn't she have forced him to take a paternity test and step up?"

Renae nodded. "She could have done that in family court and during the divorce proceedings. But she told me she didn't want to have to force someone to be a husband or a father. She was proud."

"You think that was all it was? That there was nothing to her ex-husband's claim that another man fathered her baby?" As a police officer, Clark had learned long ago to never trust what someone said or even how they acted. While Lauren had seemed concerned about Ella, he wasn't sure that she hadn't been faking that concern, that she didn't already know...

Renae shook her head. "She was so vehement that I believed her. I also interviewed the man her ex claimed was the father, and he swore they'd only ever been friends. That her ex was just a loser who didn't want to be a dad."

"Do you think he would have done something to her?" he asked. "To make sure that she wouldn't make him take responsibility and pay her support?"

"I tried to encourage her to do that, to make him help her, but she didn't want anything to do with him, and at the time, he certainly didn't want anything to do with her or their son. I didn't think he was a threat to her."

But Clark could see in the way her shoulders sagged as if she was carrying a heavy burden of guilt, that she was worried she'd missed something.

"You had no reason to," he assured her. "Unless..." The word slipped out unbidden.

"Unless what?" she asked.

As sympathetic as he was to her feelings, he also had a job to do. "Unless he had been violent with her before."

"She claimed that he had never hurt her," she said.

"And I believed her." But she was clearly wondering now if she should have.

"I'll need you to forward me your report so I'll have the names of her ex and her friend and their addresses. I need to talk to both of them." And determine which of them was telling the truth and convince them to agree to paternity testing to prove it. If they refused, he would ask a judge to order paternity tests for both of them.

"Once we get to the office, I'll forward it to you," she said with no hesitation. There hadn't been any when she'd showed it to him earlier, either. She obviously wasn't hiding anything about her investigation.

"If the father doesn't want him, where will you place the baby?" he asked. "Did Ella have any family?"

"No," she said. "Her mom died when she was thirteen, and her grandfather, who took care of her after her mom died, passed away a year ago. His name was Simon." Her voice cracked on the name.

The baby, who'd fallen asleep, murmured a small cry as if he'd recognized his name, or maybe the emotion in the CPS investigator's voice.

"Shh," she murmured. "It's okay. You're safe now." Renae cared about her job, about the children she was trying to protect…and…

She was beautiful with her long dark hair, big dark eyes and delicate bone structure. He found himself glancing into the rearview mirror again and again to look at her. While searching for and finding the baby, Clark had found something else he hadn't felt in a long time—an interest in a woman.

Despite Ann being gone two years, he hadn't had any

inclination to start dating during all that time. He'd been too focused on his daughter and on his job. But now…

Now that the baby had been found, he couldn't keep his focus where it belonged—on finding the person who'd essentially made that baby an orphan. Again, he glanced into the rearview mirror for a glimpse of the beautiful CPS investigator, and he noticed the vehicle behind him. It was far enough back that in the fading light of late afternoon, he couldn't tell what kind of vehicle it was. But he was pretty sure it was the same one that had been behind them for a while, maybe since they'd left Lauren Caufman's apartment. That concerned him, especially since they were getting farther and farther from town, from anything but the county health department building in the middle of those cornfields.

So where else could the other vehicle be heading? Clark's pulse quickened a bit, but now it was a result of his interest in that vehicle and not Renae. No. It wasn't just interest. It was concern. But the vehicle wasn't his only concern.

"So what happens to the little guy now?" Clark asked her. "Who will take care of him? A foster family?" Would that foster family be able to protect him if he was in as much danger as his mother had been?

"I wish," she replied. "We have too few foster families in this county. And the ones we do have are already over the maximum number of kids per beds right now. Nobody has the room or the resources for an infant. I'll have to reach out to some other areas, see if I can find a placement for him in another county." She turned toward the rear window, too, maybe realizing that Clark was now looking *over* her to study whatever was behind them.

The dark clouds that had hung overhead all day blackened even more as they released the rain they'd been holding back. The lights of the vehicle behind them automatically flashed on. The headlights were higher off the ground than a car. A truck? An SUV? With the rain falling heavily now, Clark could see only the lights, not the make or even the shape of the vehicle.

"What is it?" she asked. "Is someone following us?"

He shrugged. "I don't know. I should take you to the state police post, though, just in case..." If Simon had been at the crime scene, the techs would have had to process him for evidence, but Lauren had verified that he'd not left her apartment since Ella dropped him off.

While Clark wasn't certain the young woman had told the truth about everything, he hadn't been able to find any blood on the baby's clothes or his car seat. If the baby hadn't been there, why were those baby booties at the scene? Why had Ella and her killer fought over them?

Clark couldn't figure that out any more than he could decipher if that vehicle was really following them, especially when it stopped and turned off behind them. Probably into a driveway. He released a breath he hadn't realized he'd been holding.

Renae glanced out the rear window and sighed, too. "Simon and I will be safe in the office," she said.

"You'll keep him in the office?"

"We have a couple rooms made up with beds and a

bassinet, and we have a fully stocked kitchen. We even have baby formula. We've had to house kids before until we could find a placement for them."

"But *you're* going to stay with him?" he asked.

She nodded. "Yes, I have no family waiting for me at home like the other investigator and the social worker have. Like *you* have."

He emitted a soft groan. "I'm sorry about having to check on my daughter earlier—"

"Don't apologize for that," she said. "I understand. And it was just a quick call."

Too quick. His chest ached with concern for Sierra and for his mom. But he wondered if Renae would have been as understanding if they hadn't found Simon like they had, safe and unharmed.

Would he stay that way? Would she?

He glanced into the rearview mirror again and noticed some lights through the sheets of rain, but they were quite a distance behind him now. Was it that same vehicle? Or another one?

"I don't know if it's a good idea for you to stay here alone," he remarked uneasily as he pulled into the parking lot that was deserted but for two vehicles, probably both of them hers—her state one and her personal one.

He'd been inside the old building a couple of times and knew that it didn't have any security, not like the health services buildings in other areas of the state. He'd been in this one more since he lived in the area. That was why he'd been the closest to respond to Dispatch's call earlier and it was why it wouldn't take him long to get home, which was good since his aunt had sent him a few terse text messages saying she hoped he would be done working soon.

He would, and he felt a pang of guilt over that since Renae would not. All he had to do this evening was some follow-up calls to the crime techs and to apprise whatever detective took over the case of his progress, which wasn't much. But Simon…

Finding him was the most important thing. Second only to keeping him safe now that he was found. After parking the vehicle close to the front doors, he unlocked the back for her, since it had no handle on the inside, and helped her get out the car seat. Knowing it was heavy, he took it from her and followed her toward the front of the building, where an overhang stopped the rain. He ducked under it, but it was too late. Water had already saturated his hair and soaked the back of his shirt.

Her hair was damp, too, but instead of going flat, the long dark locks seemed to curl even more around her slim shoulders. She was fumbling around inside the backpack-like purse in which she carried her laptop as well as whatever else she was looking for. Maybe it was the laptop, since she'd promised to email him her report. But she pulled out a ring of keys instead, selected one without hesitation and slid it into the lock.

"I should go inside with you," he said as he peered around her into the building. Security lights glowed inside the foyer and from the hall leading off it. "I should check it out to make sure it's safe."

"The janitor always makes sure the building is empty, or that it's just me staying late before he locks up and leaves for the day." She smiled. "He wouldn't have left if he hadn't done that before locking up. I'll be fine," she said, and she reached for the car seat. Her hand brushed against his before she pulled away as if the contact had shocked her.

He'd felt it, too, a little jolt of recognition and awareness. He hadn't felt that in so long. Maybe ever. With Ann... They'd started as friends in grade school. There had been no overwhelming attraction, just deep friendship and love.

"You need to go," she said, as if trying to get rid of him. "You need to be with your daughter and your mother."

He did need to go home to Sierra and check in on his mom. But he had this niggling feeling, this worry...that Renae and the baby weren't safe.

"I live nearby," he said. "So if you hear anything or... remember something about Ella..." He reached his free hand into his pocket and pulled out a card. It was from his special stack, the ones where he'd scrawled his personal cell-phone number on the back. He turned that side toward her when he handed it over, and again their fingers brushed. That little jolt was even more intense. "My email is also on there."

She nodded. "I'll send you my report as soon as I get Simon settled. Thank you for helping me find him, Sergeant Mayweather."

"Clark," he said. "My name is Clark. I should have told you that when you told me your first name." But he'd wanted to keep things professional between them then. And now...

He still had to keep things professional. Even though

they'd found Simon, nothing had changed that much. The baby's mother had still been murdered, like his daughter's mother had been. "I need to get home to Sierra," he said, reminding himself as much as he was her. He couldn't stay here with her, like he wanted to.

"Sierra is a pretty name," she said. "She sounds like a special little girl. And after the day she had, I'm sure she needs you."

Was Renae trying to make it clear to him that she didn't need him, not like his daughter did? Maybe giving her his card with her personal cell on it had given her the wrong idea, made her think he was hitting on her or something.

She tugged the car seat free of his grasp and turned back toward the front door as if eager to get away from him. Or maybe he was overreacting and she just wanted to get the baby inside, away from the rain and settled for the evening.

He waited until she stepped inside the building and locked the door behind her and Simon before he turned back toward his SUV. He drew in a quick breath and rushed through the rain to the driver's side. Once he was inside, he hesitated a moment before starting it... until his phone vibrated with another incoming text from his aunt.

Sierra needs you.

His lips curved at the irony of her repeating what Renae had just told him. But it was true. And he needed to be with his daughter, too. After so many hours of not knowing where Simon was, if he was even alive, Clark ached to his hold his little girl, to assure himself that she was safe.

He hoped that Renae was right, and that she and Simon were safe as well. But as he backed out of the parking spot and turned to leave, his lights glanced across the side of a vehicle passing the building. Its lights were off, but before he could turn on his—the flashing ones—and the siren, the vehicle's lights came on and it continued on its way. With the heavy cloud cover, the afternoon had gotten darker than normal, almost as if night had fallen already, so it was understandable that the person might not have turned on their lights yet if they didn't have automatic ones.

It didn't mean that they were trying to avoid being seen.

That they were up to anything...

But that niggling feeling would not leave him. He wasn't as convinced as Renae Potter was that she and Simon were safe now. And he wouldn't be until Ella Sedlecky's killer was behind bars.

The cop and the CPS worker had found the baby. Following them had been easy, until the state police SUV had slowed down, as if the trooper had finally noticed he was being followed. He was gone now, though. Leaving that woman and the baby all alone.

The CPS investigator obviously couldn't be counted on to make the right decisions where children were concerned. So she wasn't going to be given the choice with Simon. She was going to lose him even faster than she'd found him.

She might lose her life, too.

SIX

Thank You, God, for keeping Simon safe. Please help me protect him from whoever took his mother away from him.

Renae silently said the prayer as she stared down at the baby sleeping in her arms. She gently rocked him in the chair in the nursery that had been set up in one of the many empty rooms in the old building. When she'd carried him inside the office, he'd woken up with cries that had almost sounded like screams. Like he was in pain. Or afraid…

She'd done everything to settle him down. Changed him. Tried to feed him. But he'd been inconsolable for a while, so long that he must have worn himself out and finally fallen back asleep as peacefully as he'd slept in the back of Sergeant Mayweather's SUV.

Clark…

His name and the way he'd said it in that very deep voice of his had a shiver racing through Renae—a shiver of awareness like the one that had raced through her every time their hands had touched on the car-seat handle. Disgusted with herself, she closed her eyes on a surge of shame that she'd allowed herself to feel anything but grief over Ella's death and Simon's predicament. How could she let herself notice how attractive the single-dad sergeant was, let alone react to it like a giddy teenager?

Please, God, help me focus on what's most important...

Simon. She opened her eyes then to peer down at the baby, but she couldn't see anything. The room had been plunged into total darkness. While the sky had been gloomy with heavy clouds all day, it had only rained. It hadn't been storming, so the power shouldn't have gone out. But the building was old, so maybe a circuit breaker or fuse had blown. If that was the case, she would need to find the electrical panel to flip the power back on, but she wasn't even sure where that was.

Basement?

A supply closet?

She hadn't worked out of this building long enough to know it well. Maybe she should call the janitor...or...

Clark.

His was the name that popped into her head, along with an image of his handsome face with its chiseled features and vivid blue eyes. He was so incredibly good-looking and thoughtful and busy.

The widowed father had his hands full with his toddler daughter and his mom getting injured. He didn't need to take on more responsibilities. She could call 911 if she needed help. There had been no reason for him to give her his card with a personal cell-phone number on it. Unless...

Was he interested in her, too? As interested as she was in him?

Maybe they were both just looking for a distraction from what had happened today, from seeing that young mother so brutally murdered.

She tightened her arms around the baby, and he murmured in his sleep, his breath soft against her shoulder. But even as her shoulder warmed, her blood chilled inside her, because she heard footsteps coming from somewhere inside the building.

She'd locked the exterior door. She was certain of it. So how had someone else gotten inside? And why?

Before sitting down in the rocking chair with Simon, she'd touched base with her supervisor and coworkers. Fortunately, her supervisor had tracked down the girl Renae had been trying to find earlier. A broken washer had led to her wearing some dirty clothes to school. Glenda would do a bit more investigating but would probably close the case soon. While Renae's supervisor had helped out with that case, she hadn't offered to take over with Simon, and neither had any of Renae's other coworkers. They were all busy with other things. With their families…

Like Clark was busy.

She didn't want to bother him, just as she'd assured her coworkers that it was fine that they couldn't help. This was why she'd decided long ago that she could never have a family of her own with her career. She didn't want to give anyone short shrift, didn't want anyone to suffer for lack of her attention or her focus.

She sucked in a breath that smelled of powder and sweet baby, and focused only on Simon. And the dark…

And the sounds…

Of footsteps.

Of a door down the hall creaking open before closing again with a soft click.

Out of habit after all the years of living in a big city, Renae automatically closed and locked doors behind herself. So the door to this nursery was closed and locked, just as she was certain she'd locked the exterior one with the key on the ring in her bag that sat on the floor next to the rocking chair. There was no way someone was getting inside, unless someone else had left their keys on their desk, which the other investigator and the ongoing social worker often did.

The footsteps got louder and closer to the room where she held the sleeping baby in the dark. The doorknob creaked as it turned but clicked as the lock held. The door rattled within the frame—whoever was out there was trying to force it open.

Renae sucked in a breath of fear, and the sudden tension in her body woke Simon. He let out a startled cry, and the door rattled again as the unknown person tried to force their way inside.

To her and the baby…

"See the bee-bee. See the bee-bee…" Sierra said in a singsong voice from the back seat of Clark's personal vehicle, a minivan with built-in DVD players. But Sierra had no interest in whatever cartoon was playing. She was only interested in the "bee-bee" she knew Daddy had been looking for at work.

When he'd come home without that baby, she'd been upset with him. He regretted that he'd mentioned his search for Simon to her, but he'd wanted to take her mind off worrying about her grandma, about the trauma she'd experienced being alone with his mother when the older woman had fallen. Not that his mom was that old. She was a very young and vital sixty-three years old and always on the go, but as she'd admitted when Clark had called to check on her, she needed to slow down and be a little more careful.

So did Clark.

What had he been thinking to react the way he had to Renae Potter? Tingling like a hormonal teenager? And giving her his personal cell number? She'd probably thought he was hitting on her, and that wouldn't be just unprofessional given the situation, the tragic murder of one of the young mothers she'd investigated—it would also be stupid on his part. The last thing he wanted was to get involved with another woman with a potentially dangerous profession. Like Ann's...

He couldn't fall for someone else only to lose them because of their job. And more importantly, he couldn't put Sierra through that loss. So driving in the dark back to the health department building in the middle of those fields was stupid for so many reasons.

But he had trouble saying no to Sierra when she really asked for so very little. She was such a sweet kid, and her concern was more for the baby than for herself right now. She wanted to see him to make sure that he wasn't lost anymore…because apparently he wasn't "found" until she saw him for herself.

A smile tugged at his lips over her toddler logic. But that was fine. While she was fussing over the baby, he would show Renae the printout of Ella's phone records. She'd sent him a copy of her report, which he'd read before he'd given in to Sierra's pleas to see the bee-bee. Renae had interviewed all of the people in Ella's world, so she might recognize who had the biggest motive for murdering the young waitress.

He couldn't imagine what that was…except for Simon. People killed over custody all the time, but nobody had been fighting Ella for custody. Her ex had divorced her because he hadn't wanted to be a father. Although her friend had insisted he wasn't the father, he hadn't wanted to submit to a paternity test, either. While Renae had noted that she'd advised Ella to go to family court and request her ex take one, Ella had refused. She hadn't wanted anything to do with him. Why? Had she been telling Renae the truth when she'd insisted he was no threat?

Ella couldn't answer that question now. So Clark needed to interview Renae more thoroughly. But the questions he really wanted to ask her were about *her* rather than Ella Sedlecky.

How long was she going to stay in the area and, more importantly, in her job? Was she going to continue putting her life in danger? She'd done so today. When he'd first arrived on the scene and had heard her scream, he'd flashed back to that day when he'd lost Ann. He hadn't responded to that call because they'd always worked different shifts, but he'd imagined it so many times…

He'd had nightmares about it. And he figured he'd have a nightmare tonight over what he'd heard and what he'd seen when he'd gone inside that trailer. Poor Ella.

Poor Renae for having seen that as well. While he respected and appreciated what she did for children, he couldn't get involved with her because she was going to be in dangerous situations so often, like the one that had taken Ann from him.

He and Ann had once discussed the horrible possibility of one of them losing the other on the job, and they'd vowed that for Sierra's sake, whichever of them survived would find a partner with a safer profession. They'd both said they'd wanted the other to go on with life— to love again but to not lose again, to not hurt again. It had been two years since Ann's passing, and until today, Clark had never been interested in even going out on a date, let alone getting involved with anyone.

Until Renae…

But she was probably already involved with someone else. Someone who must not mind that she stayed at the office. He wasn't even involved with her, and he minded. He hated the idea of her staying there alone, which was why he hadn't resisted too hard when Sierra had begged to see the baby. When he pulled his van into the dark parking lot, he was even more worried about Renae.

What had happened to the lights? Why was everything dark?

Earlier, when he'd dropped off her and the baby, there

had been lights in the parking lot and exterior lights all around the building, as well as inside security lighting in the foyer and the hallways. Night had come early thanks to the dark clouds hanging low all day, but only rain had come from them. No lightning or thunder. A storm hadn't taken out the power in the area, or Clark's would have been out at home. He was undoubtedly on the same line as the health department building. He lived that close. So close that he probably should have insisted that Renae bring the baby to his house to stay. So that he could make sure they stayed safe.

But why would they be in danger? Unless the killer had been at the scene when Ella had called Renae. That would explain how the phone had gotten broken. The killer may have taken it away from Ella and crushed it as she lay dying. The killer might think Renae had heard something that might incriminate them and had come here to make sure that she didn't have time to realize what that evidence was.

"Are we here, Daddy?" Sierra asked, her voice quavering with excitement over the prospect of seeing a baby. Maybe her obsession was just because she was so into her dolls right now. It was an obsession that his mother encouraged, with all the outfits she sewed and knitted for them. Like those booties…

The blood on the booties had scared him and Renae, had made them think that the baby might have been hurt, too. Or worse…

But he hadn't even been there…if they believed Lauren. Clark wasn't sure that he did. And she was one of the few people who knew that Renae had the baby and might have brought him here. He drove around the parking lot, shining his headlights on the other vehicles. There were still only two: the state sedan that the rain had washed the dust from, leaving it a dark gray, and the other vehicle that was probably Renae's personal one. It was some kind of luxury vehicle. Given what she probably earned as a state employee, he was surprised she would have splurged on something like that. But it wasn't his business how she spent her money. It was his business to keep her safe.

And he had a horrible feeling that he'd already failed her...

Was it too late for Renae? Like it had been too late for Ella Sedlecky?

SEVEN

The rattling door woke Simon, and he began to scream again...like he had earlier. Instead of frightening away whoever was trying to get inside, the door rattled more, and then something hammered against it.

Renae cradled the crying baby in one arm while she reached inside the bag with the other. Her fingers brushed over her laptop first. She reached past it and fumbled around until she found her phone, and she pulled that from her bag. She'd tucked Clark's card inside the phone case, and when she unlocked the phone, the light illuminated the card, which was turned to the side with his personal number on it.

"I'm calling the police!" she shouted over Simon's crying.

The noise stopped for a moment before resuming again, now more frantically, like the person knew they had only so much time before the police would arrive. But Clark had said he was close...

She punched in the numbers of his personal cell, and he picked it up almost immediately. "Clark May-weather..."

"Clark! It's Renae—"

"Are you okay?"

"No! Somebody got into the building and shut off the power, and now they're trying to get into the room with me and Simon!"

"I'm just outside," he said. "With Sierra…"

She heard a little voice calling out to him. "Daddy? Daddy? Is the bee-bee here in the dark house?"

He'd brought his daughter with him. He'd brought his daughter to danger. Renae didn't want either of them getting hurt. "Clark, send someone else."

"I'm already here, Renae." Then his voice was muffled as he murmured something to someone else, probably his daughter. Then she heard another wail. The wail of a siren.

The intruder must have heard it, too, because the rattling stopped. She heard footsteps again, but they were moving away from the door now, not closer. They were running.

She released a shaky breath. "They're leaving." They were leaving the building, but they might be running right toward Clark and Sierra. "Be careful!"

Even as she advised him, she heard a creak through the phone, the creak of a door opening and Sierra's voice as she asked, "Daddy, where are you going?"

"Clark!" Renae called out to him. "What are you doing? Call for backup. Get back in your vehicle and protect your daughter!"

"I see them running out the back," he murmured. "They're running away from the building. At least one person is…"

Could there be more than one? She hadn't considered it, but it was possible. She tensed with the fear that refused to leave her, even if the intruder had left the building. She was worried about them all. Because if there was more than one intruder, they were all in danger. She and Simon and Clark and Sierra...

The light of the van's headlights illuminated the dark figure running from the side of the building into one of the cornfields. From this distance, Clark couldn't see anything of the person's face, especially with the hood that was pulled tightly around his or her face. He couldn't tell gender or even height in the dark. He wanted to run after the intruder, to find out who'd broken into the health department, but he couldn't risk leaving Sierra alone in the car, and Renae and Simon alone in the building. There was the possibility that the intruder hadn't acted alone, or that once Clark started running after him or her, they could circle back to steal his car and potentially his daughter as well.

"Daddy, that's loud. Shut it off!" Sierra clasped her hands over her ears as the siren continued to ring out from the light flashing on his dash. It was his emergency light and alarm for situations like this, when he had to respond to a call when he was off duty.

He hadn't expected Renae to call him, not with how uncomfortable she'd looked when he'd passed that card to her with his personal cell number on the back.

"Somebody broke into the building," he said. He called for backup, but Dispatch informed him that the break-in had already been reported. Renae was on another line with a 911 dispatcher. She was smart. She'd called him first because she knew he was close, and then she'd called for help because she was worried that the intruder might come after him and his daughter.

Instead, the person was running away, and the dispatcher informed Clark that another unit was close. But not close enough to catch the person running in the cornfield. Clark was. He disconnected his call and pushed open his driver's door.

"Daddy! Where you goin'?" Sierra yelled above the siren.

Clark opened the back door, unbuckled her from her car seat and carried her quickly toward that dark building. "We're going to see the bee-bee," he told her.

He tried the front door first, but it was locked, so he hurried around to the other side—the side where the shadowy figure had emerged. He found a metal door standing open, as if it had caught on something when the intruder shoved his or her way out of it. How had they gotten inside?

"Renae!" he called out. "It's me."

"And me!" Sierra added. "Why's it so dark?"

"I'll find out," Clark said as he turned on the cellphone flashlight and used it to shine their way down a long hall, past some open doors and some closed ones. He knew he was at the right one when he saw the footprint against the metal and heard the crying from behind the door. The jamb was splintered near the lock; the intruder had been that close to getting inside, to getting to Renae and Simon.

He suppressed a shiver as a cold chill rushed over

him. The same thing that had happened to Ella could have happened to them. Had that been the intruder's intention? Was this the same person who'd murdered the young mother?

He really needed to go out there, to try to find the intruder before they got too far away…if it wasn't already too late. "Renae," he said. "You're okay. You're safe."

The doorknob rattled and then turned, and Renae pulled open the door. The beam from his flashlight illuminated her tense face and wide eyes. She looked so afraid, and so beautiful, too. And somehow, with the baby clutched in her arms, she also looked fierce and protective.

A sudden warmth spread through him, chasing away the chill. But it was probably just relief that she and the baby were okay.

"Bee-bee," Sierra said, pointing at the crying infant.

Clark swung her down from his arms and into the room. Renae had her phone light on as well. It was glowing from the seat of a rocking chair. Maybe the dispatcher was still on the line with her. "I'm going to go find the breaker box to get the power up and running again," he said. But that wasn't all he intended to do. "Backup should be here soon, so you're all safe. Lock the door, though, just in case…" He didn't want to scare his daughter, so that was all he said, but he knew Renae must already be worried that the intruder might not have acted alone. She would be careful, and he would be careful as well. He wouldn't leave the building until backup arrived.

"Clark?" Renae asked, her voice slightly hoarse, as

if she'd been crying like the child. But her dark eyes were clear as she stared at him with suspicion. She was questioning what he was really going to do.

"The other units are arriving now," he said. He could hear an echo of the siren from his van. "I'll be fine. Sierra, will you help Miss Renae with the baby?"

His daughter eagerly nodded.

He stepped back into the hall and pulled the door toward him. But before he closed it completely, he repeated his command. "Lock it behind me. Just in case…"

In case the intruder hadn't been alone, and there was someone else still inside the building. The other units were here now. He could see all the flashing lights through the windows, but he didn't want to take any chances with the safety of his daughter, Renae and Simon. But the best way to keep them safe was to find whoever was threatening them.

The killer had parked far away because of the concern that the CPS worker might see the vehicle and realize that someone was there before they had the chance to get to her and the baby.

The killer had had a chance. Had been so close.

But the cop had also gotten close.

Now the killer could hear someone moving through the cornfield, trying to track them. With all the rain that had fallen that afternoon, the ground was muddy, and sucked at the killer's boots, pulling them down, making imprints that the cop could track.

But if that trooper caught up to them, he would regret it, just as Renae Potter would soon regret that she hadn't done the right thing, that she was the reason that Ella had had to die.

She had to be next.

She had to die, too.

EIGHT

Clark had been gone a long time, leaving Renae alone with his daughter and Simon. Fortunately, he or someone else must have switched the breaker back on because there was light now. The fluorescents flickered overhead, illuminating the room she shared with the children. The light had reassured Sierra, who'd been nervous and shy despite her fascination with the baby.

Shortly after Clark left them, an officer had knocked on the door and touched base with them to make sure they were okay. She'd assured the female trooper that they were. Then, so Sierra wouldn't hear her, Renae had whispered her concern about Clark, that he might have gone off to pursue the intruder on his own.

Intruder.

Was that all the person had been? Or was it the same person who'd killed Ella?

The crime scene techs had arrived right after the female trooper, who'd told Renae that she would find Sergeant Mayweather. The techs were processing the door and hall and wherever else the intruder had been inside the building. Since he or she hadn't gotten inside the makeshift nursery, despite their attempts to open the door, the techs had said that it was fine for her and the children to remain inside the room. And they were definitely safe now, as the building was swarming with law enforcement.

While Sierra had settled down a bit since the lights had come on, Renae's nerves were still on edge, and she found herself hovering over both children. She had the unsettling fear that at any moment she alone might need to protect them from an imminent threat. Though she wasn't sure how she would even do that…

She didn't carry any weapons on her, not even a can of mace. She had nothing but a rape whistle and her cell phone for protection. And the only thing in her possession right now was the baby. Her arms were aching not because of his slight weight, but because of the responsibility she held. His small body was tense, like hers. Maybe he could sense her fear. Sierra kept pace with them, her focus on the baby. She was trying to calm him, as if she knew how frightened he was…maybe because she was still frightened, too.

Please, God, help me keep these children safe from harm.

But the person she really wanted to protect and couldn't was…

Clark.

She should have protected Ella, but it was already too late for the young mother. There was nothing Renae could do for Ella except keep her promise to save her son. But Clark was the one who'd done that. Showing up when he had with his siren had scared away the intruder before he'd managed to get into the nursery.

Please, God, protect him now like he protected me and Simon.

Clark was the one who could be in danger now. She suspected that he hadn't just turned the power back on. She was pretty sure he'd also gone off in pursuit of whoever had been trying so desperately to get inside the room, to get to her and Simon. If he'd been somewhere inside the building or nearby, he would have been back already, especially since she'd asked the other trooper to find him.

If the trooper had been able to find him, surely he would have come back now to check on them. To be with his daughter…

Renae tightened her arms around the baby as she carried him away from the door where she'd just talked to the crime scene tech, and he let out a soft cry of either alarm or protest.

"Shh…" Sierra murmured from where she walked closely beside Renae. "It's 'kay, bee-bee. My daddy is gonna keep us safe." The two-and-three-quarters-year-old sounded confident now—the slight quaver that had been in her voice earlier was gone. Maybe it was because of all the law enforcement that had arrived, or the fact that the lights were on now, or just that she'd reminded herself of how protective her father was. Unlike Renae, who hadn't been able to comfort the baby, Sierra must have reassured him, because he stopped crying and released a little sigh. The tension that had seemed to grip his tiny body drained away, leaving him limp and soft in Renae's tense arms.

Now if only Sierra could reassure Renae as well…

While the little girl was confident her dad would keep them safe, Renae was more concerned about Clark keeping himself safe. Where was he? And was he alone? Or had he taken backup with him? Had he found the killer?

Please, God, keep him safe for his daughter, for his mom, for…

Me.

Not because of that strange attraction she felt toward him, but because she couldn't lose anyone else in the violent, senseless way that Ella had died.

She didn't see a future with Clark. She didn't see a future with anyone, especially not with a widowed single father. Not when her personal time was already so limited. But so many people needed him—people like her, who didn't even know him but needed his protection. That was undoubtedly what he was trying to do now. Protect and serve was the motto of the police.

It was her motto as well. Something she wished she had always done. For Ella and for someone else— someone from her long-ago past. A sigh burned in her throat, but she held it down.

Not wanting to jostle the baby again, Renae walked past the rocking chair and the bassinet and settled onto the daybed that was against one of the walls in the room. The baby murmured again, and Sierra climbed onto the bed next to Renae and kissed his forehead.

"Shh…" she said. "It's all 'kay." Then she smiled up at Renae, as if trying to convince her that it was, too. Or maybe she was trying to convince herself as well, because those blue eyes were just a little too bright, as if tears were starting to well up again. They'd been there when the lights had first come on. The child must have been crying quietly in the dark.

Renae smiled back at her and warmth flooded her heart. Sierra, with her big blue eyes and fine blond curls, looked like a doll, but she was very human with her emotions and her empathy. Despite her young age, she was an old soul.

"You are very sweet," she said, praising the child.

"You're very pretty," Sierra said and reached out to touch one of Renae's dark curls. "Like one of my dollies…"

Renae smiled. "You're very pretty, too."

Sierra accepted the compliment with a nod. "I look like my daddy. He's pretty."

He was. But now Renae wondered what her mother had looked like, and if Sierra even remembered her. But she didn't want to upset the child by asking questions she might not be able to answer.

Because of her job, she had to upset too many kids, had to get them to talk about things they didn't want to think about much less get interrogated about… But that was one of the responsibilities of her job. To get to the truth.

She'd failed to do that with Ella. She hadn't been able to get the young mother to confide in her, to share with her whatever had been going on in her life that had led to today.

To her murder.

What had Renae missed? If she figured it out now, she couldn't save Ella, but maybe she could find the killer and keep her promise to the young mother to protect her son.

Sierra was focused on the baby again. "What's his name?" she asked.

"Simon."

"Are you his mommy?" she asked.

Renae shook her head, and tears suddenly rushed to her eyes. "No. His mother is gone."

"Like my mommy," Sierra murmured sleepily, and a yawn slipped out of her tiny rosebud-shaped mouth. "She's in Heaven."

Sympathy and something else clenched Renae's heart, and she shifted the baby to one arm so she could slide her other one around Sierra and pull her close to her side. "I'm so sorry, honey," she said, and like Sierra had kissed the baby's forehead, Renae kissed the little girl's, the silky blond curls tickling her lips.

"I got Daddy," Sierra said. "And Daddy's got me. Does Simon have a daddy?"

Simon's father hadn't wanted to be a father when the mother was alive; Renae doubted that he would want to be one now. "No. Not like you have..." Clearly, Clark was close to his daughter and took good care of her. Who would take care of Simon?

Renae had to find someone who would love and care for him like his mother had. Like Clark did his daughter...

"Can we keep 'im?" Sierra asked sleepily as her eyelids began to slide down over those bright blue eyes.

Renae smiled. "I think that might be a little too much for your father right now." An infant and a toddler…all while his babysitter was recovering from a broken ankle.

"You could help," Sierra said. "Like Daddy helped you find 'im."

Renae nodded. "Your daddy was very helpful." Then and now. She wasn't sure she would have been able to get past Lauren earlier today and take custody of the child like Clark had. Then he'd shown up here tonight, right when she and Simon had needed him most. Had that been a coincidence or…?

God's intervention. Had He sent Clark to save Renae and Simon?

Clark had already done that, so he could come back now. Unless something had happened to him?

"I can help, too," Sierra said proudly. "Like I helped Grammy when she'd fallen down. I'm Daddy's brave girl." That must be why she'd fought her tears so hard and tried to pretend like nothing was bothering her. She wanted to be what her father called her.

Sympathy squeezed Renae's heart again. The young child had had to be brave much too often, when she'd lost her mom and when her grandmother had gotten hurt today, and now her father was potentially in danger.

Where was he? And was he okay?

"Daddy is very brave," Sierra said. That slight quaver was back in her voice now. Renae wasn't the only one worried about him.

Please, God, bring Clark safely back to his baby girl…

And to her.

* * *

Where was he?

After flipping on the breakers in the basement, Clark had found the window the intruder must have broken to gain entrance. He'd gone outside to inform the troopers who'd just arrived and then headed off in the direction he'd seen that shadow take into the cornfield. While he still had his cell phone, he was using a real flashlight now to illuminate his way. He'd borrowed it from another trooper. The flashlight had a bright and wide beam—so bright that it seemed to bore holes through the stalks of corn while everything outside that beam remained dark.

Was the intruder in the darkness? Or had the person already made their way out of the cornfield and to wherever their vehicle had been parked? Clark guided the beam down from the stalks to the muddy ground between them, and to the tracks sunk deep into the mud. Big boots. Not as big as Clark's, but big.

Like the marks left on that door behind which Renae had locked herself and Simon. If Clark hadn't arrived when he had, if he hadn't turned on that siren…

He shuddered in horror over the realization that that lock might not have held much longer, not with the jamb already splintering, and what would the intruder have done to them then? Would they have done the same thing they did to Ella Sedlecky?

Clark had to find this person and stop them. He stayed focused on the tracks, on following them to wherever they led.

He knew he was putting himself in danger. But in

addition to having a flashlight now, he also had his off-duty weapon. So he wasn't unarmed like Renae had been. Just as he always had his auxiliary siren in the van, he always carried the Glock with him...for instances just like this, when he might have to step into a potentially dangerous situation.

He'd never had to use it before off duty, and he hoped he never would, especially when he had Sierra with him. But she wasn't with him. She was with Renae.

Was his little girl afraid?

Was she being shy with the woman who was a stranger to her?

Sierra had gone to her immediately, but that was just because Renae had been holding the baby. Sierra was so drawn to babies that she couldn't resist them. She had to look at them, touch them. Fortunately, the people at church indulged her, knowing that she would never hurt them. That she would be so very careful.

But Renae couldn't know that.

While she worked for the benefit of children, she had none of her own. And from what she'd revealed, it sounded like she didn't want any of her own, much to her mother's disappointment. If she didn't want any children in her personal life, he needed to make sure that his daughter didn't get attached to the CPS investigator. He shouldn't have left his toddler in Renae's care for that reason, and because she'd already been taking care of an infant.

But he'd had to act fast to have a chance of catching the intruder and making sure that person didn't hurt anyone else. Clark suspected they'd hurt—no, killed—

Ella Sedlecky. Renae had to want that person caught as desperately as he did, especially if the intruder was Ella's killer and he or she had broken into the health department building for the baby. But why? What could the person want with Simon?

Or had Renae been the target?

Clark needed to find out. He needed to catch the intruder. He quickened his pace, moving faster through the stalks, so fast that some snapped back and slapped at him, stinging his face and his arms. His shoes slipped on the mud. He was walking parallel to the trail of footprints the intruder had left in order to preserve them for the crime lab.

Maybe the techs had found some footprints at the Sedlecky murder scene and could compare them to these. Maybe they could figure out if the intruder and killer were one and the same.

Whoever that person was, and wherever that person had gone…

Clark hadn't really expected to catch them, though, not after he'd taken the time to bring Sierra inside and had gone into the basement to turn the power back on. He'd even touched base with the responding officers, making sure that they had fully secured the scene and that there was nobody hiding inside the building where Renae and his daughter and the baby were. The ones who weren't needed to maintain the security at the building were to help him search outside, in this cornfield, for the perp.

So maybe it was one of them that the beam of his flashlight caught moving among the stalks.

But how had any of the officers gotten ahead of him when he'd started out first and had been moving fast?

No. It wasn't another officer out here ahead of him. It had to be the intruder.

The killer?

NINE

The little girl either had complete confidence in her father or she'd been totally exhausted from her emotional day. She'd fallen asleep in the daybed, pressed tightly against Renae's side. Wisps of her silky blond hair touched the fuzzy black hair on the baby's head as he slept in Renae's aching arms.

Even if she hadn't been holding the baby and the toddler, Renae wouldn't have been able to sleep. She could scarcely breathe for the fear gripping her. Not fear for herself or for the kids, but fear for Clark. He'd been gone a long time.

Too long for something not to have happened...

But what?

Had he caught the intruder?

Please, God, let that be the case.

Then it would all be over. No more danger to Simon. Or to Clark.

Or had something happened to Clark?

Please, God, let him be safe and unharmed. He is the only parent left for this sweet little girl. She can't lose him.

I can't lose him.

The thought startled Renae, because it was so unexpected. So ridiculous. She'd just met the man; she certainly didn't have him. She barely knew him. But what she did know about him impressed her.

He was kind and patient and honest with his child. He was so brave and protective with Sierra, and with Renae, and with this little baby who had nobody now. Renae had to find somebody for Simon, somebody who would love him as fiercely and protectively as Clark loved his daughter, and as Simon's mother had loved him.

Even though Simon hadn't been with her when she died, Ella had still been protecting him. That was why she'd called Renae. To save her baby...

That was Renae's job—to save as many kids as she could—but she knew that would never make up for the one she'd failed so long ago. That child was why Renae had chosen this career, had chosen only to have this career.

But as she sat there cradling the baby in her aching arms, with the toddler snuggling up against her, drooling on her, she wished for a moment that she could keep them both. She'd been warned about that when she'd gone through her training—that she might get too close to some of the kids, that she might want to keep some—but in the past seven years, she had never been tempted. She'd always known there was somebody out there who would be better for them than her, somebody who would give them more of the time and the attention they deserved.

A rattle at the door drew her attention just as the knob turned. It didn't stop with a click like it had earlier this evening. It turned all the way around, and she remembered that she hadn't been able to lock it because the crime techs had been processing it for evidence.

She hadn't even realized they'd finished, or she would have locked it again. Had they left the building? Had the other troopers departed, too, including the female one who hadn't returned to let Renae know where Clark was?

Was *everyone* gone now?

No. Not everyone, because the door opened, casting a long shadow from the hall into the room, so long that it spread over Renae and the sleeping children, the darkness engulfing them nearly as fully as when the power had gone out earlier.

She tensed, ready to defend the kids, to protect them as fiercely and effectively as she could. But she remembered how Ella had tried and how she'd failed…

When Clark pushed open the door to the nursery and saw his daughter cuddled up close to Renae, who held the sleeping baby, something wrapped tightly around his heart and squeezed.

This wasn't attraction. Or love…

He didn't even really know Renae. This wasn't about her at all.

This feeling was more like grief. Like loss…because he knew *this* was what his daughter wanted most. A mother. A baby sibling. *A family.*

And as much as he loved Sierra, he wasn't sure he

could give this to her. That he could trust himself to fall in love again…with anyone. He would never let himself fall for someone who was so often in danger.

Like Renae had been tonight…

Like he might have been…

He had seen something in the cornfield ahead of him, hiding among the stalks, but then he'd heard something behind him, too. Someone had been rustling their way through the corn. That person, another trooper, had called out to him. And when Clark had turned back, the figure dressed in dark clothes had disappeared. Seconds later, he'd heard the engine of a vehicle starting up.

He'd run then, through the last of the cornfield to the road, but he'd made it just in time to see the taillights as the vehicle had sped off. And it had already been too far away for him to even identify what kind of vehicle it was for certain. He would guess an SUV from the way it was set up higher. From the way it had had no problem climbing out of the ditch where it had been parked, he figured it was also a four-wheel-drive one. When Clark had tried running out of the ditch after it, he'd slipped and fallen in the mud. The trooper who had distracted him in the cornfield had tried to keep a straight face when she'd helped Clark up. The mud was so thick on his clothes that the dampness of it had penetrated the material to leave his skin wet and cold. He shivered.

"Clark?" Renae asked in a nervous whisper, as if she wasn't certain it was him.

"Yes," he said, and he stepped farther into the room, regretful that he was probably leaving mud everywhere.

"Are you all right?" she asked with concern. "I've been worried…"

"I'm sorry," he said. "I know I was gone a long time. I didn't mean to leave you alone to take care of my daughter and the baby."

Renae glanced down at Sierra and a smile curved her lips. "She helped me with the 'bee-bee.' She's a sweetheart."

Clark's lips curved into a smile as he gazed at his daughter, too. Love and pride flooded his heart. "She is."

"What happened to you?" she asked, staring at the mud on his clothes. But unlike the trooper, she wasn't struggling to keep a straight face. Hers was tight with concern. "Did you get into a fight?"

"With the ditch on the other side of the cornfield," he said. "I slipped and fell."

"What were you doing in the ditch?"

"I tracked the suspect through the cornfield. I got close," he said, frustration gnawing at his stomach. "But not close enough to catch anything but the sight of taillights driving off. I can't even tell what kind of vehicle it was."

"Why would you go after him?" She glanced down at his daughter, clearly concerned that another child could have been made an orphan tonight.

He probably should have been worried about that as well. But he'd been armed and had had backup. "I wasn't sure I would catch up with him, anyway." But he'd been determined to at least try. He couldn't rest with a killer being loose in the county where he lived, with so many people he cared about. He'd had to do everything he could to stop them, even put himself at risk.

"And the person?" Renae asked. "Did you see them?"

He shook his head. "All I saw was a shadow—a tall shadow wearing dark clothes." He sighed. "I don't even know if it was a man or woman, but from the size of the boot prints I followed across the field, I suspect it was a man."

Renae lifted one of her feet from the floor. The short black boot was pretty big, and the sole of it bore some dried blood from the murder scene.

A pang of panic struck his heart that he might have found a scene like that here…if he and Sierra hadn't arrived when they had.

Thank You, God…

Clark didn't believe in coincidences. Sierra wanting to see the bee-bee had been such a blessing, a chance for them both to help the baby and the woman caring for him. And now Renae was caring for his daughter, too, as they were snuggled up together on the daybed.

"Daddy…" Sierra sleepily murmured as she pried open just one of her big, blue eyes and peered up at him. "Were you playin' in mud puddles?" she asked. But even though she showed some interest in him, she didn't move away from Renae. She was pressed tightly against the woman's side, her head lying on Renae's shoulder near the baby she held as well…as if she'd been protecting them both from someone trying to take them away.

A strange surge of warmth spread through Clark's chest, chasing away the last of his chill. He liked feeling like he and his family weren't the only ones who cared about Sierra, who would try to protect her. Ann's parents had died in a traffic accident before they had even talked about having children, so Sierra had only ever had one set of grandparents. And one mother who could never be replaced.

Especially not by someone who might leave his daughter and him behind if her dangerous job claimed her life, as had occurred with Ann...

He'd worried about Sierra getting attached too quickly to the baby and Renae, and it looked like it had happened already. As she snuggled closer to the CPS investigator, she looked literally attached to her, which was odd because as fascinated as Sierra was with babies, she was shy with strangers. Maybe because she wasn't often around them, since his mother usually watched her and with everyone in church being so familiar to her. She certainly didn't seem shy with Renae. Clark wasn't sure which one of them his daughter wanted to be closest to, and he wasn't sure why he was reluctant to pry her away. Sierra getting attached to either Renae or the baby was not a good idea. It would only lead to disappointment for her.

And for him...

"No, honey," he finally answered her. "I wasn't playing. I fell in the mud. We should go home so I can clean up."

"Sleepy," she murmured and closed the eye she'd propped open to peer at him. She had to be tired because of the late hour and after the day she'd had, with his mom falling and getting hurt and now all the excitement here at the health department.

"I should take her home," he said to Renae.

She tensed as if reluctant for his daughter to leave. He could understand her falling for his sweet little girl. Everyone did, even his aunt, or she wouldn't have agreed to babysit. That probably wasn't the case with Renae, though. It was more likely that she was just worried about being alone again with the baby in a building that had already been broken into once this evening.

"An officer is going to stay here with you," he assured her. "For the rest of the night." He'd convinced his boss to authorize that, but it was all the protection he could get her for now, as short-staffed as they were.

"Thank you." With dark circles forming beneath her dark eyes, she looked as tired as his daughter was. "But it's not necessary. I doubt that person will return, not after coming so close to getting caught."

"It wasn't that close," he reminded her and himself. The person had made it out of the building and across the field to a vehicle without Clark catching them. "Not close enough for me to even get a good look at them."

But coming here and breaking into the building proved how determined the intruder had been. For what?

"I have the phone logs," he said. "That's why I came here tonight."

"I thought it was because Sierra wanted to see the bee-bee," she said, her lips curving into a slight smile.

He sighed. "That, too. But I got these back." He'd wadded them up in a pocket and now pulled them out. "For a teenager, Ella didn't make many calls or send many texts. She called the Grill a number of times, as well as Lauren Caufman. And she only exchanged texts with Lauren and one other person. A Hank Chester. There were also a couple of calls to his house landline, too."

"Hank is the person her husband thought she was having the affair with," Renae replied.

"And you don't think she was?" The texts that Clark had read had been innocent, so if they'd been involved once, they had clearly only been friends recently.

"I don't know what to think anymore," she said, her voice cracking slightly.

"So you don't have any idea who broke in tonight?" he asked.

Renae shook her head, and a lock of her long hair brushed over Sierra's face. The little girl smiled even though her eyes were closed, like she'd fallen back to sleep. He suspected that was just what she wanted him to believe, so he would let her stay.

She had a cute room at home, painted pink with a canopy bed in the middle of it and shelves for all her dolls. She actually loved sleeping in her own bed and playing in her own room. It didn't look as if she'd taken even one toy from the chest in the corner here. Apparently, she'd had no interest in playing with anything but the bee-bee and Renae.

Or had she been sticking close to the CPS investigator for another reason?

He pointed at his daughter and asked, "Was she scared?" He'd been nervous about her being at the scene, but he'd trusted Renae to comfort her and keep her safe, just as she'd done with the baby during the break-in. Maybe he shouldn't have made that assumption, since she was a stranger to him. But he'd seen how upset she'd been over Ella's murder and how determined she'd been to protect the orphaned baby.

Other troopers and crime scene techs had also been around the building. They would have protected Renae and the kids from danger. He hadn't left them alone and defenseless. But Renae was the one in here with both children.

Renae smiled. "No, she had total confidence in her daddy. She believed that you would protect us."

But he hadn't even been here. He'd been off chasing down the intruder, and even though backup had arrived then, he had put himself into a potentially dangerous situation. He hadn't known if the intruder was armed, if they'd had a gun. They could have fired at him... like that gun had been fired at Ann before she'd had a chance to even assess the threat.

So much of his job was dangerous. That was why he'd switched positions to spend more time training officers than being out in the field. Like tonight. He had literally been in the field.

A pressure settled heavily on his chest as he worried that someday he might not be as fortunate as he'd been tonight, and that he could leave their daughter, like her mother had. No. If he ever got involved with anyone again, they would have to have a safe career, so that there wasn't a risk of Sierra winding up like the baby Renae held. With no parent to protect them, to love them...

The little girl didn't react to what Renae had said

about her, so he didn't think she was faking that she'd gone back to sleep. If she hadn't heard Renae, whom she was plastered against, then she was deeply asleep. So he felt free to talk in front of her.

"Do you think whoever broke in was trying to get the baby?" he asked.

Renae nodded. "There was a reason Ella asked me to save him. She knew he was in danger, like she was."

"But why?" he asked. "What did Ella say to you when she called you? Anything that would give you a clue to the identity of who—" he glanced at Sierra again, and just in case he was wrong about how soundly she was sleeping, he amended what he'd been about to say "—did *that* to her?"

Renae furrowed her brow for a moment, as if she was thinking hard, maybe trying to remember every detail of that last conversation she'd had with Ella. That she would ever have with Ella…

Before she could answer him, he added, "Because if that person thinks you know something, they will probably keep coming after you."

"Were they after me or Simon?" she wondered aloud. "Right after she asked for my help, she specifically said someone was hurting her because she wouldn't give up her baby." She glanced down at the sleeping toddler. "Something like that…"

Maybe something even more specific about how they were hurting Ella that Renae didn't want Sierra overhearing. He didn't want her overhearing that, either—didn't want her having nightmares.

"But who was after him? Who wanted custody of him?" Clark asked.

She shook her head again. "His father divorced Ella because he wanted nothing to do with him. And her friend adamantly insisted he had never been more than her friend. So nobody was fighting Ella over custody. I don't understand who wanted to take him away from her."

"There are *other* reasons someone might have wanted him," Clark said. But he couldn't say in front of his daughter that whoever was after the baby might want to kill him, like they had his mother. Maybe they wanted to get rid of him so that Ella could never change her mind about going after them for support. She couldn't change her mind now, though. She was gone. So why continue to go after the baby?

Unless the baby hadn't been the intended target of the break-in.

Maybe the intruder had been after Renae. Or both of them...

"Thank you for sending me that copy of your report and all your notes. I'm going to talk to everyone you interviewed tomorrow." Or maybe it was already today.

"I'll go with you," she said.

He tensed. "One of them could be the person who—" he glanced at Sierra again "—hurt her."

"You'll be there," she said. "You'll protect me, just like your daughter told me you would."

He couldn't protect everyone, though. He hadn't even been able to protect his wife. Of course, he hadn't been there for her because they hadn't worked the same shifts. He would be there for Renae unless...

"Maybe a detective will take over tomorrow," he said. That would probably be for the best, anyway.

Renae's mouth curved down into a slight frown, as if she was disappointed. Maybe it was just the thought of bringing someone else up to speed on the investigation that daunted her.

"I might still be here instead of there," he said and forced a smile. "It looks like my daughter isn't going to let you go."

Renae's arm was curved around her, too, as if she felt the same way. As if she didn't want to let Sierra go…

Had the trooper gotten a look at the vehicle? Even if he had, he wouldn't have been able to read the license plate. Mud—the same mud caked on the intruder's boots—was smeared all over the letters and numbers on the Michigan motor vehicle plate, completing obscuring them. But just in case the trooper had seen the vehicle, it would have to be hidden.

For now…

So there would be no tracing it back to whom it belonged. The intruder could not go into hiding, though, or someone might figure out what had happened and who they were…

TEN

This man had once loved Ella Sedlecky enough to put a ring on her finger, but Renae studied his face as Sergeant Mayweather gave him the news that his ex-wife was dead.

He didn't even bat one of his pale-blond eyelashes. Or widen his blue eyes with surprise. He displayed no reaction at all. No emotion. No surprise. No loss. No guilt…

He was using his body to block them from entering, but now he stumbled back from the door and dropped onto a chair at the kitchen table. He sat down with such force that the table shuddered, sending milk spilling over the bowl of cereal sitting on it.

Coffee also slopped over a cup sitting opposite the cereal. An older woman with thin blond hair walked into the kitchen, a robe cinched tightly around her thick waist. "What's going on? Who's ringing the bell this early?" Then she saw Clark, and her dark eyes widened. "The police? What's going on?" She turned back toward the younger man. "Tommy, what did you do?"

Did even his own mother think he could commit a

crime? Or maybe she was his grandmother. With all the lines in her face and the fine red lines in her eyes, she looked quite a bit older than him. But Tommy Moore wasn't much older than Ella had been.

Too young and too immature for marriage or to be parents. That was probably why he'd panicked and divorced her, claiming the baby wasn't his.

But even if Ella had panicked, she'd grown up fast. She'd taken responsibility for her son. She'd worked hard to take care of him. Tommy hadn't taken responsibility for anyone or anything yet.

"Did you hurt her?" Clark was the one who asked the question.

"Hurt who?" the older woman asked, and she turned back to the trooper, her face flushing with color. "Who did he hurt?"

Renae couldn't tell if the woman was flushed with anger or embarrassment.

"Who did he hurt?" she asked again, her voice sharp with impatience.

"Ella Sedlecky."

"I told you to stay away from her," she said. "That you were only going to make things worse. What did she say he did to her?"

"Killed her."

The woman dropped into a chair at the table and shook her head. "No..." She reached for the coffee cup, but her hand was shaking so badly she spilled even more of it over the sides and over the rings that had already eaten through the varnish of the oak tabletop.

"Tommy wouldn't hurt her." She shook her head. "He wouldn't..."

"She's dead," Clark said.

Tommy finally spoke, his voice quavering with emotion. "I didn't do it." Tears rolled down his face. "I didn't do it."

A lot of people had lied to Renae over the years, even before the seven she'd spent in CPS. But something about Tommy's tone, his heartbreak, made her believe him. Or maybe she just didn't want to believe that the person Ella had loved enough to get married to would have so brutally murdered her. But Renae wasn't naive; she hadn't been for a long time.

She knew women were most often killed by the person they were closest to, the most vulnerable to, especially once they'd broken up. "It's Sergeant Mayweather's job to find out who killed her," Renae said. "It's mine to find out where to place her son." Which was how she'd convinced Clark to let her join him. "He's your son, too, isn't he, Tommy?"

He shook his head, but his pale skin flushed a bright red. "He didn't get hurt?" he asked.

She couldn't tell if he sounded disappointed or relieved. It was as if he'd fallen back into a state of shock, like when Clark had first dropped the bombshell on him that Ella was dead.

And it had seemed like a bombshell to him.

"No, he's fine." At least she hoped he was. She'd had to hand off some of her cases so that she could focus on finding a placement for Simon as well as help Clark find the killer. None of her coworkers had been able to watch him, and while she'd agreed with Clark that it wouldn't be right to bring him along while they questioned potential suspects in his mother's murder, she'd been nervous about leaving him with Clark's aunt and Sierra. Clark's aunt had once been a foster parent, so Sierra's supervisor had approved, and Clark had insisted the kids would be safe at his house until they returned. She'd driven the baby over to the two-story farmhouse with the wraparound porch where Clark lived with his daughter.

As he'd said, it wasn't far from the health department, and a trooper was going to be patrolling the area to make sure nobody tried to break into his house. Not that anyone could. He had a security system, something he'd apparently installed after he and Sierra moved out here after his wife died.

He'd shown it to her, as if to reassure her. She wasn't reassured about anything right now, especially him. Her reaction to him unsettled her, just as her reaction to his daughter had. Sierra had rushed up to hug Renae the minute Clark had opened the door to her and Simon. Then the little girl had pressed a kiss against the baby's forehead, and Simon, who'd been so fussy since they'd found him at Lauren's, had let out a soft gurgle that had sounded almost like a giggle. His mouth had curved slightly, and his dark eyes had shone.

It was almost as if he'd recognized Sierra from the night before and knew that she'd offered him comfort. She was a special little girl, so much so that Renae had been almost as reluctant to leave her as she'd been to leave Simon.

But that was just because of the potential danger. It couldn't be because she was getting attached to them.

She drew in a shaky breath and focused on Simon's potential father. "I'll need you to take a paternity test."

"You can see he ain't my kid. He's got dark hair and eyes, and Ella and me are both…were both…blond and blue-eyed."

"Then take the test to rule you out," Clark suggested.

Tommy's mother—or grandmother?—snorted. "Rule him out as the daddy or the suspect? Whaddaya up to, Trooper?"

Tommy glanced nervously at the older woman. "Whaddaya mean?"

"They think you killed her," she said. "He's gonna use your DNA to try to prove it."

"And if he didn't do it, he has nothing to worry about," Clark said.

"I didn't do it," Tommy insisted.

"Then take the test," Renae urged him.

"What if the kid is his?" the woman asked. She turned toward Tommy. "Your mama was born with black hair and dark eyes. Then the hair all fell out and came back blond, and her eyes turned blue at around six months."

Tommy's face paled then. "I—I don't want a kid."

"I sure don't," the woman said, her hand still shaking as she tried to raise the coffee mug to her mouth. "I raised mine and your mama's. I ain't raising yours, too."

"You can give him up," Renae said. "But in order to sign over your parental rights, we have to find out if you have any."

Tommy drew in a shaky breath and nodded. "Okay. But you better get Hank's, too. He's really the father."

Maybe he actually believed that, because he let her swab him.

Once they were in Clark's SUV heading to Hank's, Clark said, "I don't think he would have given up his DNA if he was the killer. Not that we could use it since he only submitted it for the paternity test."

"Maybe he doesn't think he left any DNA at the scene, or if he did, he can excuse it because he used to live there," Renae said.

Clark sighed. "The crime scene techs are processing what they found. But unless it was under her nails, it'll be hard to prove it belonged to the killer."

"It'll be the same situation with Hank," Renae warned him as he followed the directions on his GPS to the next address from her files.

"He lived with her, too?"

"On and off, when his mother kicked him out," Renae said. "Hank Chester was staying with her and Tommy, but she and Hank both swore nothing happened between them. Tommy was just looking for any excuse to get out of being a father."

"Simon deserves better than someone that immature and selfish," Clark remarked.

The baby deserved someone like Clark, who clearly doted on his daughter.

Clark looked across the console at her with a strange, intense expression, and she felt a tingling sensation of extreme awareness. That was how she always felt in his presence. Before she could ask Clark about that strange look he'd given her, he was pulling up beside a farm-house. This one wasn't as nice as his. The porch was sagging and nearly falling off, and most of the paint from the wood siding had been stripped away, prob-ably from age and weather. The unprotected wood had begun to rot.

She hoped that Ella had been telling the truth about Hank not being the dad, because she couldn't imag-ine Simon living here. But as she'd told Clark at Ella's home, being poor didn't make someone an unfit parent.

"Ella and Hank were friends since they were little kids," she told Clark. "They were like brother and sis-ter. There's no way he's Simon's dad."

"She shared a lot with you," Clark said. "You must be very good at your job."

Tears rushed up, and she bit her lip and shook her head. "If I was, she wouldn't be dead."

Clark reached across the console and touched her hand. "It wasn't your fault. It's really hard to tell what someone else is capable of."

"Or even if they're telling the truth," she said. She was happy to take a back seat and let Clark do the in-terviews now. Maybe people were less likely to lie to a police officer than they were a CPS investigator.

They stepped out of the SUV and crossed the porch to the door, where Hank's mother was already waiting for them. "Why are the police here?" she asked. "You find my husband?"

"Is he missing?" Clark asked, his long body tense. His hand hovered near his holster.

She nodded. "A couple of years now. Took off with my truck and all the money from my bank account."

"I'm not here about your husband," Clark said.

The woman glanced at Renae. "You look like Arnie's type, honey. You here about him?"

"I'm here about Ella Sedlecky," Renae said. "I talked to your son about a month ago. I saw you briefly." The woman had refused to speak to her then.

She shook her head. "That Tommy Moore is spreading a bunch of lies about him. Hank and Ella grew up together. They're like brother and sister. He ain't that boy's daddy."

That was what Ella had said as well. But just as Clark had mentioned, it was hard to know what the truth really was...about anyone. Renae had learned that long ago herself.

"Then we'll have a paternity test rule him out," Clark said.

"If she's looking for money, he ain't got none. She knows that. She helped him out more'n I can afford to."

"Ella's not looking for money," Renae said defensively. All she'd been looking for was the peace to take care of her son, to provide for him and herself on her own. And someone had taken that opportunity away from her. It wasn't fair. But Renae had learned long ago that life wasn't fair.

"What's going on?" a male voice asked, but the person wasn't behind the woman. He was behind them. He'd come up from the direction of the barn, and his sudden appearance had Clark putting his hand on his weapon and turning toward him.

All the color drained from the guy's face, and his dark eyes widened in shock and fear. "What is it? What do you think I did?"

"Ella Sedlecky is dead," Clark told him.

"Dead!" the woman exclaimed.

Tears began to roll down the young man's face. "No…" He shook his head. "No… That dang Tommy. He killed her."

Usually, the guilty party was the first to point the finger, but Hank's sorrow looked real. But maybe there was guilt mixed in with the grief. His mother came out of the house and wrapped her arms around him, trying to console him.

"He went crazy when she got pregnant, wanted nothing to do with a kid," Hank said. "I know he blames me, but I wouldn't have done anything to hurt Ella. All she ever did was help me."

"Help her now," Renae urged him. "Submit to a paternity test so we can rule you out as Simon's daddy."

He shook his head. "It's not me."

"Tommy submitted to a paternity test," Clark said. "And he's pretty sure he's not the father, either."

Hank shook his head again. "He's gotta be." But he didn't sound quite as certain as he had moments ago. Maybe he figured Tommy wouldn't have agreed to the test if there was a chance the kid was his.

"I told Tommy that if the baby is his, he can sign away his parental rights and give him up for adoption." Renae had no doubt the only reason Tommy had agreed was because he wanted to give up Simon. Was that all he wanted to do? Or did he want to permanently get rid of his child with his ex-wife?

"Take the test," Hank's mother advised him. "Prove that Tommy Moore is a liar and a lowlife, like his whole family. He has to be the one that killed that poor girl."

Hank shook his head. "Ella had something else going on…at work…"

Renae furrowed her brow. "What was it, Hank? You were her best friend. You must know."

Thinking of best friends made Renae think of hers… of the one she'd lost so long ago. Like Hank had just learned he'd lost his…

Tears continued to stream down his face. "I don't know. She wouldn't get specific. Just that she knew something she shouldn't, and that she didn't want to get in the middle of any drama with the Caufmans, between her bosses and their daughter-in-law, Lauren."

"You don't have any idea what it was?" Renae persisted.

"Ella was loyal to everyone," Hank said. "Whatever she knew, she didn't want anyone to get hurt, so she figured the fewer people who knew, the better. I think she was trying to protect Lauren."

"From what?" From the same fate she'd suffered? Murder?

Lauren didn't even know that Ella was dead. They hadn't told her yesterday. Could she be in danger, too?

Clark kept glancing across the console at Renae. She'd been so quiet since they'd left Hank Chester's farm. Maybe she was just worried, like he was, about

Lauren Caufman. He was driving toward her apartment in town now, but since they couldn't do anything until they got there, he tried to get Renae talking. "We got DNA from both of them," he reminded her. "We'll be able to use that to determine paternity."

She nodded. "I know. It's more than I managed a month ago."

"Getting those paternity tests sooner wouldn't have kept Ella alive," he said. "In fact, it might have gotten her killed sooner...if not wanting financial responsibility for the baby was the reason she was murdered." But if Ella had gotten involved in something she shouldn't have, they had another possible motive.

"I just keep thinking I failed her," she admitted. "That I missed something."

"She told you a lot," Clark reminded her. "So I think she would have told you if she'd known then that she was in danger."

"She didn't tell me what she told Hank, about the situation with the Caufmans," she said.

He regretted that he hadn't interrogated Lauren yesterday, that he hadn't told her about her coworker's murder and watched for her reaction, like he'd watched the two young men. But as concerned as Lauren had been about Ella not showing up, he'd figured she hadn't known what had happened to her or why. That she didn't know any more than they had yesterday.

"It might not have been a situation then," he said. "Which would mean that you didn't miss anything, Renae." He reached across the console and touched her hand again. Like earlier, he felt that jolt of awareness and attraction.

Instead of accepting his comfort, she pulled away. "I'm worried about Lauren."

He was, too. "We're almost there…"

Just a few minutes later, he steered the state SUV onto the cracked asphalt of that old parking lot. Knowing now where the stairs were, he drove fully around the pizza parlor to the back. But even before he parked near that industrial fan underneath the stairs, he could see the door gaping wide open at the top.

This late in fall, it was too cold to leave doors open. And with a recent murder and a break-in in the area, it was also unsafe. He parked the car and reached for his holster as Renae gripped her door handle.

"No," he told her. "You need to stay here."

"Clark, we've been through this before. I—"

He pointed to the top of the stairs, to that open door swaying back and forth in the wind, and she gasped.

"Stay here. I'm locking the doors."

He really wished that Lauren Caufman had done the same. He didn't want to find her like they'd found Ella the day before, but he had a bad feeling that once again they were too late.

Unless that door was open because the killer was still here…

He pushed open his driver's door, but before he could step onto the cracked asphalt, Renae reached across the console and grabbed his arm.

"Be careful," she whispered, as if she was afraid

that the killer could hear her over the roar of that industrial fan.

That was probably why Lauren hadn't heard whoever it was approaching. Renae had heard the footsteps the night before and known that someone was out there trying to get her and Simon.

Lauren had had no warning. And if the killer was still here, they would hopefully have no warning that Clark was coming. That he was determined to catch them.

ELEVEN

Please, God, let Lauren Caufman and her baby girl be okay.

When long moments passed without Clark returning, Renae said another prayer aloud in his car. "Please, God, keep Clark safe from harm."

She hadn't heard a gunshot, but the killer hadn't shot Ella. The young mother had been stabbed. And the thought of that happening to Clark...

She opened the passenger's door and stepped out into the parking lot. It was still morning, so nobody was coming and going for the take-out pizza yet. There was no one around. She tilted her head to listen for any sounds coming from that apartment, but she heard nothing except for the rattling of the industrial fan.

"Clark?" she called, but she barely heard herself over the noise of that fan and her own madly pounding heart. Was he okay? She had to know, so she tentatively headed toward the metal stairwell. She climbed up a few steps and called out again for him.

Finally, he appeared in that open doorway. He'd holstered his weapon again, so there must be no threat inside.

"Are you okay?" she asked, anyway, just in case he had an injury she couldn't see. Or in case he'd seen something she didn't want to see. Because she needed to make certain he was all right, she climbed the rest of the stairs and joined him in the open doorway.

"I'm fine," he said. "She's gone."

And her pulse quickened even more. "Dead? Like Ella?"

He gestured inside the open door. "Gone. As in not here…"

"Maybe she just left in a hurry for work or…" But then she peered around him at the things strewn across the floor. Clothes. Papers. Cupboard doors had been left open like the front door had been. Drawers had been pulled out. "Was she robbed?"

"I checked Dispatch for any reports or calls from this location." He shook his head. "Nothing."

"But it didn't look like this yesterday when we found Simon here."

"No, it didn't." His jaw was clenched, as if he was holding something back.

"What?" she asked. "What did you find?"

"Some blood," he said.

She peered around him again, but when she started inside, he moved closer to her, blocking the doorway. His sudden closeness had her heart racing. Unsettled by her reaction to him, she stepped back. "Where?" she asked.

"In the bathroom," he said. "Not much, not like…"

"At Ella's?"

He shook his head. "It might be nothing. But I want to get crime scene techs out here."

"But if there was no call, maybe she just left in a hurry," she suggested. She *hoped*. "Maybe we should go to the restaurant and check to see if she's there. She might have had to go in to pick up Ella's shift."

Ella couldn't work it anymore. Ella couldn't hold her son, couldn't watch him grow up. It wasn't fair, but Renae had learned long ago that life wasn't fair. "Ella was the day-shift waitress," she reminded Clark.

"And the cook probably isn't going to want to try to handle the morning crowd on his own," Clark said.

The bar was one of the few places open for breakfast in the area. And the retirees, in particular, liked to hang out there after or before their fishing trips.

"Even if she isn't there, maybe Greg or Bobbi Jo know where she is. Maybe we can find out what Hank was talking about. Find out what Ella had learned about them…"

He nodded and pulled the door closed. The lock clicked.

If Lauren had left on her own, why hadn't she shut the door behind her? Did she leave in such a hurry? And where was her daughter?

Please, God, let me them be safe and unharmed…

But there had been blood…

Whose blood?

Clark had an uneasy feeling, and it wasn't just about the scene at Lauren Caufman's apartment. The mess and the blood had him concerned, but it wasn't just that…

When he and Renae had gotten back into his SUV, she reached across that console again and asked him to call his aunt, to check in on the kids. And for a second, he'd imagined that the kids were theirs, that they were a couple out on a date with a babysitter at home.

But that wasn't the situation at all. His aunt reminded him of that the moment she answered his call, which he'd regrettably put on speaker so that Renae could hear her, too.

"Clark, I have things to do. You're going to have to find a real babysitter. I can't cart two kids around on my errands with a trooper following me. Why is there a trooper parked outside, anyway? What's going on?"

He wished he knew, wished he could figure this all out. "Aunt Kelly, I appreciate you pitching in, and I am working on finding another sitter. The trooper is just keeping an eye on things because last night there was a break-in nearby."

He'd only requested drive-by surveillance until he'd found that door open at Lauren Caufman's. Then he'd called in on his radio, and requested the trooper just stay parked outside his house until he knew if there had been another victim. Maybe someone had thought Lauren knew something about Ella's murder, like who had murdered her. Or maybe Ella had been murdered because of whatever she'd found out about the Caufmans, whatever she'd alluded to when she spoke with Hank Chester. If he'd been telling the truth...

"This place is Fort Knox," Aunt Kelly remarked. "Nobody's breaking in here. And with that trooper outside, I feel like I can't break out. I retired from teaching for a reason, Clark. It used up all my patience for kids, which is why I never had any of my own. If it weren't for Sierra, this baby wouldn't stop crying."

Renae emitted a soft gasp, and her hand went over her heart, as if it ached for the little boy. She definitely cared about him. But then, if she didn't like kids, she probably wouldn't do what she did for a living.

A twinge of sympathy for the infant struck Clark's heart, too. The poor kid had to miss his mom. After talking to people about Ella, it was clear that she was all the baby had had. She was the only one who'd cared about him.

No. Not the only one.

Renae cared too. She'd investigated that complaint about Ella neglecting him and found evidence that exactly the opposite was true. And when Ella had called for help, Renae had rushed to do just that. She was very good, and not just at her job. She was a good person.

"Clark? Are you there?" His aunt's voice emanated from the cell.

He'd let thoughts of Renae distract him, and right now, with the danger she and the baby were in, he couldn't afford any distractions. "I'm here, Aunt Kelly."

"Home?"

"No," he said. "Not yet."

"You need to come home, Clark," she said. "This was a bad idea, and I'm not talking about just me. Your little girl was already obsessed with babies, but this... She's fallen hard for this one. She's getting attached, and that's not a good idea. What happens when his family claims him?"

Would anyone claim him, though? The man who was probably his father had only agreed to the paternity test so that he could sign away his rights to his child.

But Aunt Kelly was right. It was a bad idea for Sierra to get attached. Even if no one else took Simon, Clark couldn't. If he hadn't had his mom's help, like he always did, he would have struggled to raise Sierra on his own...just like he was struggling now.

"I'll be home early today, Aunt Kelly," Clark assured her. Though he wasn't sure that was actually going to be possible. He had to find Lauren and her child, to make sure they were okay and find out what Ella had learned about the Caufmans.

When he clicked off his cell, Renae apologized. "I can go and pick up Simon now," she offered. "It's too much to impose on your aunt like this."

"After being a teacher all these years and a foster parent, I thought she could handle it."

"But those were children, not babies," Renae pointed out.

He sighed. "True. But I'm the one who imposed, not you." He'd hoped Aunt Kelly would want to help, like she had when she was a teacher, but maybe she was still burned out, even after retiring. "We're close to the restaurant. Let's go there, like we planned, and then we'll figure out what to do about the kids."

"I guess Simon's not the only one who needs a placement."

Clark sucked in a breath as if he'd been punched. "I would never give up my child."

"That's not what I meant," Renae said, and she reached

across the console to touch his arm. "You're an amazing dad. You'll never have to worry about CPS. I was just talking about day care."

He released the breath in a shaky sigh and nodded. "I know. I'm just…" He cleared his throat. "I've been blessed having my mom help me all this time. I don't really know how Ella managed alone."

"She had no choice but to figure it out. She was a strong young woman. Not only was she raising Simon, but it sounds like she was also there for Hank, her best friend."

"Best friend," he repeated, with the almost reverent emphasis Renae had placed on it.

"I just wish she'd shared with him whatever she'd learned about the Caufmans." Renae glanced toward that staircase that led up to the ransacked apartment.

Something had happened there. They both knew it, but neither spoke of it. Silence reigned in the SUV as Clark drove it the short distance to the Coral Creek Bar and Grill. He wondered if Renae was praying… like he'd been praying. That they would find the young mother safe and unharmed here. The bar was open for breakfast, and even though the morning was slipping away, the place was full. But it wasn't Lauren running around. There was an older lady swinging a coffeepot across patron's cups.

"Bobbi Jo?" Clark asked.

Renae shook her head. "No. I don't know who she is."

"My wife," the cook said through the window separating the bar from the kitchen. "I wasn't getting stuck here alone again."

"Where's Lauren?" Renae asked.

He shrugged. "She's not due in until this afternoon, but she didn't show up yesterday. She probably can't find anyone else to watch her kid."

"How do you know that Ella can't watch Lauren's baby?" Clark asked. He hadn't told anyone here at the restaurant that Ella was dead. He'd been careful to hold back that information. "Or that she won't show up here today?"

The guy popped his head back into the kitchen, and Clark pushed open the swinging door to go inside, to catch him next to the griddle. He was flipping pancakes, not running for the back door. When he glanced up from the stove, his face was flushed, and Clark didn't think it was just from the heat. "She's dead, ain't she? That's what you were really doing yesterday, being all sneaky about it, though? Like we didn't have a right to know."

"Someone knew," Clark pointed out.

The killer…

"Who told you?" Clark asked.

The guy glanced nervously around the empty kitchen. "I—I just heard it."

"Who told you?" Clark repeated.

"Bobbi Jo," the guy sputtered.

"How did she know?"

He shrugged. "I don't know. She found out from someone yesterday. Probably one of your coworkers. This is the only real place to eat for miles around, and she was waiting tables last night."

It was possible that a crime scene tech, maybe even the one who'd picked up Ella's truck from the alley, had stopped in to eat and revealed the reason why they were in the area. He suppressed a groan of frustration and focused on the clearly nervous cook.

"Where is Bobbi Jo?" Clark asked. "Or Greg?"

The guy shrugged again. "I don't know. I'm busy here."

"Do you need a hand?" a woman asked as she pushed through the swinging door behind Renae, who was quiet.

She'd been great about following his lead during the interviews when, as a CPS investigator, she probably had as much or more experience interviewing people than he did. She'd proven that when she'd asked Hank the questions that had yielded them the most information...that something was going on with the Caufmans.

"This is Bobbi Jo," the cook said, pointing his spatula at his boss.

The woman was nearly as big and muscular as her husband was. Maybe they worked out together. Her hair was cut short in a no-nonsense pixie style and dyed a bright yellow. Maybe she was trying to emulate that personal trainer who'd been so famous when Clark was a kid.

"Officer," she greeted him. "Were you looking for me?"

"Sergeant," Clark corrected her. He wanted her to know that he wasn't here about a parking ticket, and that he had authority to ask her the questions he needed to ask. "I'm actually looking for your daughter-in-law and granddaughter."

She grimaced as if disgusted at just the mention of

them, which was an odd reaction, at least about her grandchild. "Sergeant, Lauren works in the afternoons, so I expect to see her around one…if she can find a sitter. Yesterday she couldn't find one."

"Apparently, you know why that is," Clark said. "How did you find out about Ella's death?"

"Lauren told me yesterday," she replied, "when I called her up to ask why she wasn't at work yet."

But they hadn't told Lauren, either. Lauren must have guessed, though. She'd seemed to know that something bad had happened to Ella for her to be away from her son that long. And when they'd taken the baby, she'd been certain, but neither he nor Renae had revealed that she was dead. She could have just been hurt.

How had Lauren been so certain that it was worse than that? That Ella wasn't just in the hospital? Ella had called Lauren about the truck tires, just like she'd called Renae. What had Ella actually told Lauren? Had she known who had slashed them? Or had Lauren known because it had been about her, about whatever was going on with her and her in-laws?

"We need to find your daughter-in-law," he told Bobbi Jo. "Do you know where she might be?"

The woman shrugged. "At that little dumpy apartment she rents above the pizza place probably. She doesn't have a car of her own. Just that old truck of Ella's she borrows sometimes."

"That truck is in the state-police impound lot right now," Clark said.

The woman shrugged again. "I don't know where she went, but it can't be far then."

"We were just at her place, and she was gone," Clark said. "Looks like she left in a hurry and might have packed up her stuff."

The woman's blue eyes got hard with anger, and she clenched her jaw. "She took off?"

"You have no idea where or why she would have left?" Clark asked pointedly.

"My daughter-in-law and I are not close."

"Is that because you called CPS on her?" Renae asked the question, her voice sharp.

Bobbi Jo turned toward Renae and glared at the younger woman before snorting. "For all the good it did me. You all refused to do anything about her. Just closed the case…"

"My boss investigated," Renae said. "And found no signs of neglect or abuse. Why did you report her?"

"My son is deployed right now, but his wife won't take his calls. And when Lauren should be home watching their daughter, she's out gallivanting around. That's no kind of wife and mother."

"She has no vehicle," Renae reminded her. "How is she gallivanting anywhere?"

"Ask Ella Sedlecky. Oh, that's right, you can't. She's dead," the woman said with no empathy or remorse.

Clark's blood chilled at her coldness. Had Bobbi Jo killed the young mother?

"No wonder Ella mentioned to a friend that she hated being in the middle of your family drama," Renae remarked. "Are you the one who called CPS on Ella, too? Trying to start trouble for her like you did your daughter-in-law?"

"Ella was a good mother," Bobbi Jo said. "And unlike Lauren, she gave her husband a boy. Too bad Tommy Moore was too stupid to appreciate her."

"Did you?" Renae asked. "I thought you were upset with her for helping Lauren go out?"

"That wasn't all I was upset about," Bobbi Jo admitted. "Money's been missing around here. If Ella didn't take it, she knew who did."

Clark nearly whistled through his teeth, impressed with how much information Renae had gotten out of the restaurant owner. Clearly, there was something going on around here, and Ella had been entirely too involved in it.

"Where is your husband?" Clark asked. "Maybe he knows where your daughter-in-law and granddaughter are."

She nodded. "He probably does. She can fool him. Not me. I know she's no good and my son deserves better. If Greg isn't with her and that little girl, he's probably working out. The meathead is always working out."

"What gym?"

"We have one in a barn on our property," she said. "Not far from here."

The back door to the alley swung open, and Greg walked in almost as if on cue, or because he'd been hanging around outside listening. "You're back, Sergeant," he said. "Going to tell us what really happened to Ella now?"

"I'm trying to figure out that myself," Clark said. "That's why I'm here."

"I thought you were looking for Lauren," Bobbi Jo

said. "Do you think she offed Ella? She might've…if Ella got sick of covering for her."

"Covering for her?" Greg asked. "What are you talking about?"

His wife laughed, bitterly. "Obviously you still are covering. How far would you go to do that?"

Greg's brow creased as he frowned at her. "I don't know what you're talking about. I don't know where she is. And I don't know what happened to Ella, either."

"What about the money?" Clark asked.

Greg's face flushed. "What money?"

Bobbi Jo crossed her arms over her chest and glared at him. "Like you don't know…"

"I don't know."

"You're a lying—" She said some more things, terrible things, and looked as if she was about to swing at her husband, but Renae was between them.

"Stop!" Clark yelled. "There's one way to settle this. Let me have someone look over your books and figure out what happened to that money."

"This isn't your business any more than it was Ella's," Greg said.

"Ella's dead, and if it was because of whatever is going on here, it is definitely my business," Clark insisted.

"Get a warrant, and until you have it, get outta here," Greg told him, jerking his thumb toward the door to the alley.

They'd come in the front, but Clark wanted to get a look at what the Caufmans drove. So he reached out for Renae and guided her between both of the restaurant owners, who looked as if they were about to come to blows.

Once they were in the alley, she released a breath of relief. "That was intense," she murmured. "I can see why Ella wouldn't have wanted to be in the middle of it."

"I'm sorry you were part of that," he told her. He shouldn't have brought her along on his investigation, but she really did have better interviewing skills than he did.

"I've been in intense situations worse than that," she assured him.

"But is it something you get used to?" he asked.

She shook her head. "And I don't want to get used to it…"

The heavy feeling he'd had in his chest lifted a little. "You're not going to stay on with CPS?"

Her dark eyes widened as if she was surprised he would think that. "Oh, no, I'm not leaving my job… much to my mother's disappointment. I just don't ever want to stop caring, to stop being affected."

"What about caring too much?" he asked, thinking about how protective she was of Simon, how possessive.

She stared back at him, her dark gaze intense. "I didn't think it was possible to care too much…"

"Didn't? You've changed your mind?"

She smiled, but it barely curved her lips and didn't reach her eyes. "Are you interrogating me now, Sergeant?"

"I have a lot of questions I'd like to ask you," he admitted. He had the sudden urge to shiver, and it wasn't just because the temperature had dipped down after that rain the day before. It was because he had a strange sensation, like they were being watched. He glanced toward the screen door to the kitchen and noticed a shadow there. A big shadow…

It could have been either of the Caufmans.

He turned his attention away from the restaurant and to the vehicles parked in the alley. There was a truck and a big SUV, and both of them were covered in mud. Either one of them could've been the vehicle he saw pulling out of that ditch the night before. He wasn't sure who they belonged to, but they hadn't been there the day before, when he'd found Ella's truck in the alley, so neither belonged to the cook.

That left Greg and Bobbi Jo Caufman.

"We need to find Lauren," Renae said, her voice shaking a bit with nerves. "I'm afraid that something's happened to her."

"So am I," Clark admitted. But he wasn't sure if she was in danger or if she had been the danger to Ella.

"She must know what happened to Ella," Renae said. "Who killed her and why. Maybe Ella said something when she called her yesterday…"

The killer might think the same thing had happened during the phone conversation between Ella and Renae, when the young woman called the CPS investigator while she was dying. Maybe that was why her phone had been smashed.

If Lauren wasn't just missing, if she was dead, then the killer was tying up loose ends, and that left Renae. Clark was even more afraid for her than he was for Lauren.

* * *

The killer just had to wait for them to leave the restaurant. Had to wait for them to leave and follow them... hopefully right back to that baby. And if either of them got in the way this time...

The killer had a gun now and knew how to use it.

TWELVE

Renae was anxious to get back to the baby, to make sure he was really all right, that he wouldn't go missing again…like Lauren and her child were missing now. She leaned forward in the passenger's seat as Clark turned the SUV into his driveway. "I'll take Simon back to the office," she said. "Watching a baby and Sierra was too much to ask of your aunt."

The minute Clark neared the farmhouse, the older woman stepped onto the front porch as if she'd been watching for his return.

"Did something happen?" she wondered aloud, nerves overwhelming her. "Did someone try to get in?"

He pointed toward the state cruiser with the female trooper sitting inside behind the wheel. "No. It's just Aunt Kelly…"

She'd said earlier that she felt trapped in the house with both kids. "I guess I shouldn't ask her if she wants to renew her foster-parent status?"

Clark chuckled. "I think she'd say no as fast as Greg did to my offer to have someone look at the restaurant's books."

"What is he hiding?" Renae mused.

"Lauren and his granddaughter, or embezzlement from his own wife?" Clark asked. "I'm going to dig up everything I can about the Caufmans."

"Good."

She needed to push open the passenger's door and step out, but she was reluctant. And it wasn't just because of his aunt impatiently waiting on the porch. She knew she had to leave Clark and return to the office. And for some reason…she wanted to stay.

Maybe she was just using him as a distraction from what she had to do, from finding a placement for Simon. She couldn't keep him in the office indefinitely. And even though Tommy and Hank had consented to paternity tests, it was clear neither of them intended on exercising parental rights. So she doubted either of them had killed Ella…unless they'd thought she was going to force them to give her financial support. Maybe because of the issues at her job, she had intended to quit and needed the money.

"I find it hard to fathom anyone hurting someone else," Clark said, as if he'd been pondering the same things she had. "No matter how many times I've seen it. I just can't imagine getting that mad or losing control like that…and taking away someone's life, someone's mother, someone's…"

"Best friend," she murmured.

He sighed and nodded. "Then my wife was murdered, and I was filled with such anger. Such hatred."

Renae couldn't imagine Clark, who seemed so calm and together, being so bitter. She reached across the console to touch his arm. "I'm so sorry. Was her killer not caught?"

"He killed himself after killing her, but it didn't feel like justice. It felt like he'd eluded it, but with him dead, I had no place for that anger but God."

She sighed. "I've been mad at Him a lot myself... for all the horrible things that He seems to let happen."

"My pastor reminded me that God gave us all free will...to make the right decisions and the wrong ones. Letting go of that anger and focusing on the good, on *Sierra*, was the right decision."

He was so strong, so spiritual, so perfect, that the anxiety inside Renae increased. Panic pressed on her chest, and it was hard for her to draw a breath. She didn't want to fall for anyone. Ever.

She had too much to do, too much to make up for...

Desperate to get away from him, she pushed open the passenger's door and stepped out. "I need to get Simon. Your aunt said he was crying a lot." He probably missed his mother so much. Her heart ached for him. She rushed up the steps to where the older woman waited on the porch. "Is everything all right?" she asked. "Is Simon okay?"

"He's sleeping like a baby," the woman assured her. Then she glanced at Clark. "Sierra is even taking a nap now. Must have been a late night for her."

Clark flinched a bit. He must have been feeling guilty for bringing his daughter into that potentially dangerous situation last night. She couldn't blame him. She felt guilty that either child had been there. She needed to find a safe foster home for Simon.

"Now that you're back, I'm going to leave," his aunt continued.

"But, Aunt Kelly, I'm still on duty," he reminded her.

"Your mom is on her way over with your stepdad," she said. "She insists that she's feeling better, and she wants to see Sierra." She turned to look at Renae again and smiled widely, a kind of Mona Lisa smile, like she knew something that Renae didn't. "And the baby..."

Did Clark's mom want to see the baby or Renae? What had his aunt told his mother about her? She felt a little shiver of unease. "I need to get Simon and go," she said. She already had one meddling mother of her own to deal with, although she wasn't being quite fair to assume that Clark's mom was a meddler, too. She might just really like babies, like her granddaughter did. "I really need to get back to the office."

"I'll help you get his things," Clark said, as if he suddenly wanted to hurry her up. Apparently, he didn't want her meeting his mother, either.

Not that she could blame him. They'd just met, and their relationship was a professional one. That was all it could ever be. She had to remind herself of that when he opened the door for her and then guided her upstairs to the nursery that was already set up. When Renae had arrived earlier today, Clark had shown it to her and told her that it had been Sierra's, and when she'd gotten older, he'd just moved her into the room next to it, the one he'd painted pink and decorated befitting a princess. He clearly loved his daughter very much. Even now, he peeked into her room and smiled at the sight of her sleeping under the pink canopy of her bed.

There was such love in his eyes and on his handsome face that Renae could almost feel it. That was what she wanted...for Simon. The baby deserved that—deserved to be loved like that. She forced herself to look away from Clark and step inside the nursery.

Simon released a soft sigh in his sleep, drawing her to the crib. Despite the sigh, he appeared to be sleeping soundly. His face, with its delicate little features, was relaxed, as if he'd finally found some peace or comfort.

Please, God, help me find him a home where he will be loved like Clark loves Sierra.

"You know what they say about sleeping babies?" a deep voice asked in a low rumble close to Renae's ear.

She shivered at the whisper of Clark's breath stirring her hair. "What?" she asked.

"Don't wake them," he said.

She smiled and turned to him, and the look on his face had knots tying in her stomach muscles. He was so handsome. "I probably sound like a broken record, but I really need to get back to the office," she said. Mostly, she needed to get away from Clark.

"You could leave him here," he suggested.

"Do you really want Sierra getting any more attached to him?" she asked. She'd overheard his conversation with his aunt earlier. Kelly was right that it wasn't smart for the little girl to fall so hard for the baby, that it would hurt her not to see him anymore.

He sighed. "No, you're right. You two need to go."

"Ouch, tossing us out, eh?" she teased. "I have a feeling that you don't want me to meet your mom."

"Let's just say that Sierra isn't the only one obsessed

with bee-bees," he replied. "She'd love to have more grandchildren."

"Only child?" she asked.

He nodded. "You?"

She nodded.

"It can be kind of lonely growing up like that," he said.

She thought of Faith and shook her head. "No, I had a best friend who was like my sister. We spent so much time together."

But not enough. They should have had so many more years together, the rest of their lives.

If only Faith had spent that night at her house, like she so often had…

"Had?" he asked. "You lost touch?"

"I lost Faith." And no matter how many years had passed since then, the pain still ached inside her, leaving that hollow feeling that had never gone away.

Clark had to ask. He could have excused his curiosity as being force of habit after questioning so many people the past couple of days. But Renae wasn't a suspect in Ella's murder or Lauren's disappearance. And this question had nothing to do with either of them.

The look of loss and pain on her beautiful face affected him, made him want to close his arms around her and protect her. So maybe he shouldn't have asked. But as much as he didn't want to hurt her, he had a need to know more about her, a need that went beyond curiosity.

"How did you lose faith?" he asked. He had lost his for a bit…until his pastor had helped him remember all the good that he'd been blessed with.

Renae didn't answer, and her throat moved as if she was choking on something.

"What happened? What are you talking about?" he persisted.

Her throat moved again, and she managed to whisper a reply. "Losing my best friend. Her name was Faith."

"Did your family move away? Or did hers?" he asked, but he knew neither of those were the answer.

Especially when she turned to him with tears sparkling in her dark eyes. She released a shaky breath. "After all these years, I should be able to talk about this…" She drew in another breath, steadied herself and continued, "We were twelve when she died. We'd been friends since preschool. Best friends. The kind of friends who finished each other's sentences. And I thought we didn't have any secrets. But there was something she kept from me, lies she told me…"

"What?" he asked, but there was a sick feeling in the pit of his stomach, a suspicion, a certainty, regarding what the little girl's secret had been.

"She always had bruises, but everybody just said she was a klutz. She did fall down a lot. But I think that was because she was so often hurt. Teachers never suspected anything. I never suspected anything…until the day she told me…" Her voice cracked, and she closed her eyes for a moment. "I didn't understand everything she shared with me. My parents were so loving and also a bit overprotective, so I was sheltered. I didn't realize things like that happened until she told me that her dad was hurting her. Badly…"

"What did you do?" he asked.

"She told me not to tell," she said. "She told me he would kill her and me if I told anyone." Her voice cracked. "I wish I'd told…"

"What happened?"

"She didn't come to school, so I went over to her house afterward. She lived close to my house, but she usually came over to mine. Even though I didn't go to hers that often, I knew where the key was hidden…and I found her. It wasn't as bad as how we found Ella, but it was bad. And once again, I was too late…"

"Oh, Renae." He did reach for her then and wrapped his arms around her in a comforting hug. "To find that at twelve years old…"

"To lose her life at twelve years old," Renae said, blinking back the tears. "It wasn't fair. And you know… even if she'd told, I'm not sure anyone would have believed her. Her dad was rich and powerful. Owned a business that employed a lot of people. People might have turned their heads to the abuse. Well, people probably had…because there was no way everybody missed those bruises." She sucked in another breath and pulled back from him. "But he's in prison now, where he belongs, where he should have been long before Faith died."

"That's why you do this," he said. "Why you're a CPS investigator?"

She nodded. "Yup. I couldn't save my best friend— or Ella—but I'm going to try to save as many others as I can."

Knowing that, knowing why she did what she did, Clark realized she would never give up her job, and he could never ask her. Just like he would have never asked Ann. But he also knew that because he'd lost Ann, he couldn't risk his heart, or Sierra's, on another woman whose career put her life in danger.

"I understand," Clark said.

"You lost your best friend, too?"

He nodded. "My wife. We were friends like you and Faith. We grew up together. We told each other everything. All our hopes and dreams. All our secrets."

"I'm sorry, Clark."

He had a feeling that she wasn't talking just about the loss of his wife. That she knew as well as he did that, despite this awareness between them, there was no future for them.

There were two cops here, so it shouldn't have been so easy. But there'd been even more at the health department the night before, and nobody had gotten close enough to catch the killer.

And nobody would…

While the female trooper helped the woman on crutches up porch steps to the front door, the killer helped themselves to the tires of all the vehicles in the driveway but one. Coming out of a cornfield like the night before, it was easy to crouch down and move between the vehicles without being seen. Even if the trooper had some kind of security system, the cameras would be mounted on the house. And it was far enough from the drive that the picture wouldn't pick up much more than a figure dressed all in black and with a face mask.

Careful to not make it as obvious, as it had been with Ella's truck, the tires weren't all slashed. Just one small gash in one on each of the vehicles. Just small enough for the air to drain away and leave that one tire flat. Even if they all had spares, it would take some time to put one on. They wouldn't be leaving quickly. Like the woman was leaving now...

Juggling both the car seat with the baby and her bag, the CPS investigator rushed out of the house as if she knew she was being pursued. And maybe she was being pursued...because the trooper followed her out.

He didn't stop her, though. He just watched as she got in her vehicle. The killer got in theirs. It was parked inside a field, and a gun was lying on the passenger's seat, easy to grab. Easy to fire...

Maybe this would be used to stop the CPS investigator's vehicle instead of the knife. To stop the CPS investigator from interfering any more in the plan...

THIRTEEN

Renae was reeling. She wished she could blame it all on Ella's murder, on someone breaking into the health department last night...on any of the things that would make sense for her to be upset about.

But she was reeling because of Clark. Because she'd shared too much of herself with him, and he'd shared too much of himself with his late wife. A friendship. A love...

It was no wonder he was still single. He could never replace the wife he'd lost in his life and definitely not in his heart. He hadn't said it, but he hadn't had to.

He understood Renae. He'd told her that when she'd talked about losing Faith. She had never replaced Faith. She'd never had another friend like her, one with whom she'd been so close. She'd never shared as much of herself as she had with Faith.

Until today.

Today, she'd told Clark about Faith. She hadn't talked about her in years. Renae's mom was really the only one who knew how much her best friend's death had affected her then and affected her still. While Renae's dad was a good man, he wasn't very emotionally available. He worked hard and took care of his family, but he didn't talk about his thoughts and feelings, and he didn't encourage anyone else to talk about theirs.

Maybe that was why her mom was so upset that Renae had moved farther away and had sworn she'd never get married or have kids. Because Renae was all her mother had. Clark's mother had Sierra.

She hadn't gotten away fast enough. Mrs. Summers, as Clark had introduced her, had arrived before Renae had made it to her car. Gayle, as Mrs. Summers had introduced herself, had been so sweet and friendly. Maybe a little too friendly. She and her sister, who hadn't left, had exchanged some looks. Pointed glances...

Ones her mother used to give her when she introduced Renae to some eligible bachelor at one of her charity parties. Those were the only parties her mom, Phyllis, was able to talk Renae into attending. Her mother hosted parties to benefit abused and neglected children. Phyllis really was a sweet person, like Clark's mom.

Gayle had offered to sit for Sierra and Simon and to help Renae in any way that she could, but Clark had interrupted to remind his mother that she was supposed to be taking it easy.

Renae had taken advantage of the interruption to hurry out the door. She'd only slowed down to make certain she correctly secured Simon's car seat in the back before she'd jumped in the car and sped off down the driveway. She was so rattled that she'd turned the wrong way and headed away from the health department instead of toward it.

This was why she needed to stay single. Just being attracted to a man was too distracting. She had a job, responsibilities. She was responsible for Simon, for his safety, and she had to keep her promise to his late mother. She had to protect the little boy.

And find him a good home.

Please, God, help me keep Simon safe.

She'd rushed away from the house so quickly that she hadn't checked to make sure the trooper was behind her. As she slowed down now, looking for a driveway, somewhere to turn around and head back to toward the health department, she looked for the trooper's vehicle. It wasn't there.

Maybe the trooper hadn't noticed her turn the wrong way. Maybe the woman had headed straight toward the health department, thinking she would catch up to Renae. Renae needed to catch up with her...because she had a sudden horrible fear.

Being alone on this country road, she felt so afraid. But she wasn't alone. She had Simon. Simon to protect. Simon to save...

Please, God, help me get him back to safety.

She didn't feel safe now. She felt so discombobulated, as she often did after talking about Faith, after reliving that nightmare from her childhood, the nightmare that had ended her childhood.

Finally, there was break between the fields that lined the road, like they had Clark's driveway. It was a beautiful area, and usually she loved being out here, away from the city, surrounded by all the farmland and the creeks and inland lakes. That wasn't all she loved about this particular area, though. She loved Clark's farmhouse, too. Loved the homey, comfortable feeling of it, the solidness and security of it—it was old, but it stood strong.

She didn't need a house. She barely spent any time at all in her apartment, and if she was there, it was just to sleep. But she could imagine spending time in Clark's house, rocking in the wooden chairs on his wraparound front porch. Watching Sierra and Simon…

She blinked her eyes, as if trying to clear away that image, like she'd tried to clear away her tears over telling him about Faith. Poor Faith. Renae had let down her best friend all those years ago. She couldn't let anyone else down again.

Please, God, help me focus on what matters most, on the kids I can save, unlike Faith and Ella.

She pulled onto a little turnout off the road, backed up and headed in the right direction—back to work. But as she passed Clark's driveway, she slowed down, tempted to turn in there. To go back…

But Clark was a temptation that neither she nor Simon could afford right now. The cost of her being distracted was too high. And she couldn't lose anyone else. Especially not Ella's precious baby boy.

She glanced into the rearview mirror, but with his rear-facing car seat, she couldn't see his cute little face. She heard him making some kind of noises, like he was blowing raspberries to amuse himself. He was a sweet baby; anyone would be blessed to have him. She had to find a home and a family that he would be blessed to have. And again, she thought of Clark's farmhouse, of Clark…

She pushed the image from her mind and focused on the road again. She was getting closer to the health department. But not close enough to see it yet. Nor did she see that trooper's vehicle. But something else suddenly appeared on the road in front of her. There was a vehicle that should have been in the other lane because it was headed in the other direction. But it was in her lane, coming straight at her.

And it was big, some kind of truck or SUV.

She pressed her horn, hoping the loud blast would wake or sober up the other driver, but Simon was the one who cried, letting out a loud wail. Renae wanted to cry, too, because the person wasn't swerving back into their lane. They were speeding up even as she braked. If she didn't do something, they would hit her head-on.

But who were they? She could see them behind the wheel now. Big. Dressed all in black…even a mask.

The intruder from the night before.

She grasped the wheel hard and swung it, propelling the car into the ditch. It hit hard, so hard that the hood popped open and crumpled up, moving toward the windshield. Then the car tilted even more, sliding deeper into the mud, and her scream echoed Simon's.

"Clark, what are you trying to do?" Aunt Kelly asked as she pulled open the screen door and strode back into the house. "Keep me here against my will?"

"What are you talking about?" he asked.

"Sergeant!" the trooper interrupted as she ran up the porch steps, panting for breath. "I started following Miss Potter down the driveway when a big truck barreled out of the cornfield and cut me off. I went off in the ditch alongside your driveway." She must have run the whole way back, as sweaty and out of breath as she was.

"Are you okay?" he asked.

She nodded.

"We need to catch up with them." He rushed past her and Aunt Kelly, down the stairs to the driveway.

"One tire is flat on every vehicle, Sarge," the trooper warned him. "Someone must have let the air out of them."

Someone. The killer. It had to be. It must be whoever slashed the two tires on Ella's truck. Two, because she probably would have had only one spare.

Clark wasn't going to take time to mess with his spare because he had a sick feeling that Renae and Simon didn't have that kind of time. He had to get to them quickly...before the killer did. The rims on police vehicles didn't stop because of flats. The vehicle could keep going. Not far, but...

Renae might not be far, either.

Please, God, make sure she and Simon are safe. Protect them like I should have...

He jumped in his SUV and peeled out before the other trooper could join him. The tire slapped against the gravel of his driveway, sending a spray of tiny pebbles flying up behind him in the direction of the trooper who'd followed him down the porch.

She would call it in, if she hadn't already. His total focus right now was on finding Renae and the baby before it was too late. Before the killer did to her what he or she had done to Ella…and maybe Lauren as well.

Please, God, make sure that they're all right…that they're not hurt.

Or worse.

He should have followed her to the health department. Should have made certain that she arrived safely. She hadn't been safe there last night. Maybe she wasn't going to be safe anywhere until this killer was caught.

Clark had to catch the person, had to stop them from hurting anyone else. Like Renae and Simon.

Please, God…

He turned on the siren and lights. Maybe he could scare off the killer, like he had the night before. If he wasn't already too late…

He pressed harder on the accelerator while gripping the steering wheel tightly. The vehicle pulled toward the flat, dragging him toward the ditch, where the trooper's vehicle was tilted at such an angle that one of the nonflat tires was up in the air. Fortunately, she hadn't been hurt.

He hoped the same was true for Renae and the baby. They were the real targets of this brutal killer. Why?

Renae had told him over and over again about her conversation with Ella. The woman had said nothing to reveal her killer's identity, but that must not be what the killer believed. Or maybe it was really all about Simon, about taking him away from Ella even now, after her death.

Whatever the motive, they were both in danger.

Maybe Renae more than Simon, because she was going to do whatever she could to protect that baby, to save him, as she'd promised his dying mother. Even if she gave up her life for his...

His heart beating fast with fear for her, for them, he spun out of the end of his driveway, turned toward the health department and nearly rammed into the front of a big black truck that had stopped on the wrong side of the road. Was it this truck that had barreled out of the cornfield and run the trooper into the ditch? It could be the one from the alley behind the Coral Creek Bar and Grill, but in Michigan, there were only license plates on the back of vehicles, and he couldn't see this one's.

He was more concerned about Renae. Then he noticed that next to the truck was the back of a dark car, extending from the ditch. The front of it was buried deep in the mud and earth, and its wheels weren't even touching the ground. He could see that back license plate and knew it was a state vehicle. Renae's state vehicle.

He couldn't see anyone around it or around the truck. Had this just happened?

Using the radio on his collar, he called it in and requested backup, wishing now that he'd stopped for the other trooper to jump into the vehicle with him. But maybe his family needed protection, too, since this person now knew where he lived.

He must have followed them back from town. How had he missed it? And where was the driver now?

Even though Dispatch warned him to wait for backup, Clark opened his driver's door. As he did, a shot rang out, glancing off the metal near his head. He ducked down as he raised his weapon, training it on the truck. Where was the shooter?

Where was Renae?

He wanted to call out for her, wanted to make sure that she was all right. That she hadn't been shot...

Fear and dread gripped him with the thought of her dying, like Ann had. But he hadn't heard a shot before the one fired at him, like the ones that continued to be fired at him from the gun barrel pointed out the window on the driver's side of that big black vehicle.

Using the door for protection, Clark returned fire, striking the windshield of the truck until it shattered in a spiderweb. The person inside was a blur of black clothing. Even their face was covered today. Maybe it had been the night before in the cornfield. Maybe that was why the person had been so hard to track, but for the prints left in the mud. But they hadn't had the gun the night before...or if they had, they hadn't taken the time to fire it.

They were firing now, though.

But the gun clicked, emptied of bullets.

Clark had a few more, and he raised his weapon. But before he could fire again, the truck suddenly slammed into Reverse and sped off backward down the road. He couldn't follow them...couldn't stop them until he checked on Renae and Simon.

Until he knew if they'd survived.

Please, God...make sure they survived.

Had the killer had time to hurt them...or take Simon?

Was that the motive for all of this? Was the person just trying to take Ella's baby, as she'd told Renae?

Simon's cry cut through the sudden quiet following the gunfire and the truck engine, and Clark released a shaky breath.

He sounded terrified, not hurt. Clark wasn't sure how he knew the difference, but it was like when Sierra had been a baby, and he'd learned which cries were because she was wet or hungry, and which were because she missed her mom.

Simon must miss his mom. Would he be missing his CPS investigator now, too?

"Renae!" Clark called out, his voice hoarse with the fear choking him. The truck was out of sight now, so he holstered his weapon and headed toward the vehicle, his heart hammering against his chest with fear for her. "Renae!"

He could see shadows inside the vehicle, but nothing moved.

Please, God, let her be all right.

His shoes slipped on the muddy bank as he headed into the ditch, and he reached out to grab the side of the sedan. The back door had been opened—the door where Simon's car seat was facing the rear. Renae was good at buckling them in, and despite the crash, the seat was secure.

Simon was secure, but someone must have tried to get him out. Maybe someone that hadn't known how to disconnect the belts that were wound through the car seat. Or they hadn't had the chance when they'd heard his siren.

Or…

Renae had fought them off. She wasn't in her seat. He peered into the front, to where she was lying back against the dash, her hair across her face. She must have gotten out of her seat, must have fought off the assailant, fought to protect Simon.

Had it cost her her life?

Please, God…

The front of the car was crumpled into the ditch, so her door wouldn't open. He leaned across the car seat, over the console and reached for her, trying to check her pulse. He pushed aside her hair and it fell away from her face…away from the wound on her forehead. Blood trailed from it onto the dash.

Had she been shot?

His hand shaking, he reached for his radio again. "I need an ambulance, too, at this location."

"Are you hurt?" the dispatcher asked.

"No. But Miss Potter is." And he had no idea how badly. As badly as Ann had been hurt?

But then he felt her neck and found a pulse, weak… but steady. For now. How long could she hang on? He didn't want to move her. Didn't want to risk hurting her more.

Then he heard it. The sound of another engine. Had the truck returned?

Was the killer going to try again to get Simon?

Clark drew his weapon and turned toward the street. He would defend and protect the baby and Renae with his dying breath.

He wondered if Sierra would remember him…

She didn't remember her mother, wouldn't have known who she was in the pictures Clark showed her if he hadn't told her.

Please, God, save us all...

FOURTEEN

The baby was gone.

Just like Ella.

Just like Faith.

Renae awoke with a start. A scream rose up from her throat, slipping out through her open mouth. While her eyes opened, she couldn't see anything but a blinding light. Was it the killer?

Was he coming back for her?

He'd taken Simon. He'd had to have taken him. She'd tried to fight him off, swung out with the laptop from her bag, striking his head and his shoulders, trying to stop him from getting the car seat loose.

Until he'd pulled the gun on her and struck her…

And everything had gone black.

She almost preferred that to now. To the bright light, to the pounding in her head and the pain. Not the physical pain…

The emotional pain of knowing that she'd failed again.

"Simon…" she murmured.

Please, God, don't let that monster hurt the baby, too.

She'd promised his mother that she would save him. But she hadn't. Tears leaked out with her guilt, with her regret.

"Shh…" a soft voice murmured. "Shh, you have a concussion, baby. You need to rest."

"Mom?"

Finally, the light dimmed as her mother leaned over the bed…smiling down at her. But her eyes were red and swollen. She'd been crying.

"Mom? What are you doing here?"

"That nice man called me. Sergeant Clark."

"Clark?" If he was here, he would know what happened to Simon. If he wasn't here, then he was probably looking for him again…without her. "Where is he?"

"He's in the waiting room with that adorable little girl of his."

"Sierra?" Why would he have brought her to the hospital?

She touched her head where pain persistently throbbed near her temple. "What…? How long…? What's going on?" But none of that mattered. Not like Simon. "And where's the baby?"

"Clark has him."

Her breath shuddered out with relief while more tears streaked from her eyes, running down the sides of her face. Her mother's warm hand touched her face, brushing away her tears like she had so many times, especially after Faith's death.

Renae just wanted to curl up on her lap like she had then, feeling so safe and loved. But then she'd felt guilty because she'd been so safe and loved and her best friend hadn't been. And she'd done nothing to help her. She had to help Simon and Ella. "I need to see him," she said.

"Clark?" her mother asked, almost hopefully, her dark eyes brightening.

Renae wanted to see him, too, wanted to talk to him, to find out what had happened and tell him what she remembered. And just to see him...

But there was someone else she wanted to see even more. "The baby," she said, her heart aching for him. She had to see him to make certain that he was okay. That she hadn't failed him like she had his mother and Faith.

"Doctor, can she have other visitors?" her mother asked, turning her attention to someone else in the room.

Renae had been so upset that she hadn't really assessed where she was and what was going on. Without the bright light in her eyes, she looked around now. At the hospital room...

It wasn't just a bay in the ER. She'd been admitted. A gray-haired doctor in scrubs and a white coat stood on the other side of her bed across from where Renae's mother hovered over her. Phyllis Potter was so fierce, so protective, even more so after what had happened to Faith.

Renae's best friend had spent so much time at their house that Phyllis had called Faith her second daughter. She'd been as devastated and guilt-ridden as Renae had been when they'd lost her.

"What's wrong, Doctor?" Renae asked. "What happened?" She remembered the gun. Had she been shot?

"You took quite a blow to the head. You were unconscious for a few hours."

She'd had to have been, because it would have taken her mother that long to make the drive up north from River City.

"You have a severe concussion, but the fact that you've regained consciousness and that you were always breathing on your own with strong vitals points to a full recovery."

But one colossal headache. She didn't want to admit to how badly her head was throbbing, though, because she wanted to leave. "Can I go home?" she asked. "Now that I'm awake?"

"We were going to keep you overnight for observation, to make sure you don't develop any swelling or bleeding."

On the brain. She knew how often people died after a blow to the head. She'd worked some cases where a child had died after a parent had battered them and they'd seemed fine…but for the hidden head injury.

She'd lost more than just Faith and Ella. But those children she hadn't been assigned to help until it was too late, until they'd already been hurt and dying. She needed to protect Simon before anything happened to him. "Was the baby checked out?" she asked. "Is he all right?"

He was most important.

The doctor nodded. "Yes, he's fine. Healthy set of lungs on him for certain."

"But we went in the ditch…"

"The sergeant said he was still buckled in securely when he arrived at the scene," the doctor said. "We did a full checkup on him, including collecting DNA for the pending paternity tests, and he's fine. He's been well taken care of."

Just like Renae had ruled a month ago. Ella had taken good care of her baby. She'd loved him so fiercely that she'd given up her life for him. Renae had to honor that life. She had to protect Ella's baby.

She released a shaky breath of relief, but it was short-lived. The baby was still in danger. And still without a family or even a placement in a foster family that would keep him safe.

"I need to be released," she told the doctor. "I need to take care of that baby." Because there was nobody else to do it.

"You need to rest," her mother said.

"I'll see if we can get you in for another CT," the doctor said. "Make sure that nothing's swelling or bleeding." He pushed open the door to step into the hall.

"But, Doctor—"

"I'll be right back," he promised as he let the door swing shut behind him.

Renae tried to lift her head from the pillow, but it felt heavy, and frustration overwhelmed her. "I need to take care of Simon."

"Don't worry about him," her mother said. "You need to rest and heal fully."

"He has nobody else," Renae said, her voice cracking with desperation for him. To keep him safe. To care for him…

"He's with the sergeant right now. He's taking care of him."

"But he's not an approved foster parent."

"I am," her mother replied.

"What?"

"You're always harping on about how there aren't enough homes for kids in need, and I—"

"But Dad would never agree to that," Renae said. While he was a good dad in a lot of ways, he had never been a hands-on dad. He had probably never really wanted kids, but he'd agreed to give Renae's mother one child. Or maybe, with her busy law practice, that was all Phyllis had wanted as well.

Phyllis smiled. "Don't worry about your father. Don't worry about anything right now but yourself."

"I can't do that," Renae said.

Her mother's smile slid away, and she sighed. "You never could. You and that big heart of yours."

Renae reached out and covered her mother's hand, which was wrapped tightly around the railing on the bed. "I get that from my mama."

Her mother leaned down and softly kissed her head, but just the brush of her lips had Renae flinching. She must have taken quite the blow. Maybe that was why she wanted so desperately to see Clark, and not just to talk to him about what had happened but to see him.

"Please, Mom, get the sergeant. I need to talk to him."

Her mother's smile reappeared, sparkling her dark

eyes. "He is good-looking and so good with his daughter and that baby…"

"Mom," Renae murmured. "Don't try to matchmake." Like she always did.

Phyllis Potter chuckled as she headed toward the door.

Did she not have any idea how serious this was? What was going on? Renae had no time for romance now. If she hadn't been distracted earlier, she might not have wound up in the ditch, might not have gotten hurt and risked Simon's life as well. She had to stay focused on what mattered—on her job.

Clark had been watching the door to Renae's room, so he saw the doctor leave. He thought about stopping him to ask questions, but he had no legal right to any information about her condition. Sure, he could have said he needed to know as part of his police investigation, but his interest in Renae wasn't purely professional even though that was all it should be…for his sake and especially for Sierra's.

He couldn't believe his aunt had brought her to the hospital. She shouldn't be here. And the baby shouldn't be here. But Aunt Kelly had refused to help out anymore and had said that his mother had done too much in making the trip out to his house, that her leg was swelling and she needed to be off it longer. He could have pointed out that she was the one who'd convinced his mom to come to the house. To meet Renae?

What did they think was going on?

What did her mother think?

She stepped out of the room now and headed straight toward him. With her dark hair, delicate features and tall height, she looked like an older version of Renae. Beautiful. Strong. Determined. And he wasn't exactly sure what she was determined to get.

Renae wanted to protect as many kids as she could, especially Simon. But her mother should only want to protect Renae…and after what had happened to her, he totally understood.

When she'd arrived at the hospital, she'd been distraught, terrified for her only daughter. He could relate. He would have felt the same way if something had happened to Sierra. And when he'd told her that, she'd hugged him.

Right now, she paused for a moment, her back against the door to her daughter's room, her eyes closed. It looked as if she was breathing deeply or praying.

He understood that as well. He prayed so often himself…for so many things. Right now, he guessed that they were praying for the same thing, that her daughter would be all right.

Please, God, make sure Renae is okay…that she'll recover fully.

Her mother opened her eyes then, forced a smile and walked over to him.

"Are you okay?" he asked her. "Is Renae?"

She nodded. "She's trying to get out of here, and she wants to see this little guy." She touched the fuzzy hair on Simon's head, which was nestled against Clark's shoulder.

"Whadda 'bout me?" Sierra asked and stared shyly

up at the older woman. Aunt Kelly really shouldn't have brought her here. The little girl had been scared since her arrival. Or maybe, as empathetic as she was, she was picking up on his fear...for Renae.

"And, of course, she wants to see you, too," the woman said. She was probably lying, but she clearly didn't want to hurt his daughter's feelings, and he appreciated her consideration.

He wanted to make sure that she wasn't lying to him, too, though. "Hey, honey," he said, addressing his daughter. "Why don't you finish that pretty picture you were coloring for Miss Renae? That will definitely make her feel all better."

Sierra was like Renae—she liked to help people—so she nodded and headed eagerly back to the table where his aunt had put her crayons and sketchbook.

He waited until Sierra was absorbed in her picture before he turned back and asked Mrs. Potter, "Is Renae really all right?"

She hadn't regained consciousness at the scene of the accident or for hours after she was here at the hospital.

Mrs. Potter nodded. "She's awake now. The doctor is going to do another CT scan, and if it's good, I think he'll let her leave. But she wants to talk to you and see the baby. She's terrified for him."

After what had happened, she had every reason to be. Clark was scared for him, too. Fortunately the vehicle he'd heard back at the scene had been the other trooper arriving in his mom's car after she'd changed the tire. The ambulance had taken a little longer to arrive, with Clark juggling the baby and his fear while he waited.

But he hadn't dared to move Renae, hadn't wanted to hurt her any worse than she'd already been hurt.

"I'll keep him safe," Clark promised.

"She said that you're not a registered foster parent, though," Mrs. Potter said. "I am, but I have no place to care for him. Renae's apartment is a studio with not enough room for even a portable crib—"

"Come home with me then," Clark suggested. "You and the baby and Renae, if she gets released." He really hoped she'd be released. It would be easier for him to keep them all safe if they were together. Because of the limited financial means of his county, there weren't any safe houses to bring them. There wasn't even a jail nearby, not that a baby could be kept at a jail.

The killer was the one who belonged there. He must have followed Clark home from the Coral Creek Bar and Grill and had been hiding in that cornfield. This time, Clark would be more vigilant. He'd have more troopers watching the house, and he would make sure the security system stayed on the entire time. With that high-tech system, his place was probably the safest place in the county. He would make sure nothing else happened to anyone he cared about.

"I'm not so sure my stubborn daughter will agree with you," Mrs. Potter warned him, her lips curving into a slight smile.

"I won't give her a choice," Clark promised. "I will put them both into police custody."

His custody.

But before he could start toward her room, the doctor

was back with an orderly and a gurney, and Clark realized he might be the one with no choice in the matter.

If she wasn't well enough to be discharged

If that concussion was as serious as he'd feared it was...

The killer was fortunate they hadn't wound up in the hospital tonight themselves. Some of the bullets the trooper had fired had come close—too close...

The windshield was broken now. And the trooper had gotten a good look at the truck this time. But it was tucked back away, hidden...just as the killer was hidden in the shadows of the parking lot of the hospital.

Watching...

Waiting...

Renae Potter had been stupid to fight for the baby. If she wasn't dead, she should be. The killer should have shot her instead of just hitting her with the gun. But they'd been so close to the trooper's house, and the killer hadn't wanted to draw his attention by firing the weapon.

Hadn't wanted to get caught. That couldn't happen... because then the plan would be ruined even more than Renae Potter had been ruining it. Everything that the killer wanted would slip away...

FIFTEEN

Renae awoke again to darkness and confusion. Where was she? The last time she'd awakened was in the hospital, to that bright shining light and her mother. And the doctor...

He'd run another test and had begrudgingly agreed to release her if she was closely monitored for the rest of the evening. Then Clark and her mother had double-teamed her in the hospital room, saying that staying with him was the only way to keep her safe. She knew he had the best security system and would have more troopers watch the place. But she was still worried about everyone else: Sierra, Simon and her mom.

And most of all, Clark. She wanted to trust Clark to protect them, the way his daughter had trusted that he would that night at the health department, but Renae was afraid to trust anyone. And Clark wasn't superhuman. A bullet could stop him, just like one had stopped his wife. That was what scared her the most; that in trying to keep them safe, he would lose his life.

She jerked fully awake then.

"It's 'kay," a voice murmured in the darkness.

It wasn't her mom this time. It was someone much younger.

"Sierra?"

A small circle of light appeared in the bed, coming from the end of a flashlight in the little girl's hand. She was curled up on her side next to Renae in the queen bed. It was in the guest room on the main floor. That was where Clark had helped her to the bed, his arm around her as if he'd thought she was going to pass out again. She'd felt a little shaky, but that might have been from his closeness as much as from the concussion. The room, and the bed, were big enough for her and her mom to share, since she was the one who was supposed to be watching over her.

Not a two-and-three-quarters-year-old little girl. Her heart contracted with affection for Sierra. "What are you doing here?" she asked her.

"Mrs. P is busy with the bee-bee, and you were 'lone in here. I don't like to be 'lone when I'm sick."

So she'd crawled into bed to keep her company. "You are very sweet," Renae told her.

"That's what Daddy says then he tries to bite me, but I runned away…"

Renae chuckled. She'd had teachers report things like this to CPS, not realizing that the parent was just teasing, and she was sure that was the case with Clark, that he wouldn't do anything to hurt his child. But why bring her and Simon and her mother here?

Despite his security system and extra officers, he was putting Sierra in danger, too. In danger of getting more attached to all of them…

Renae couldn't help herself. She reached out and pulled the little girl close for a hug. "Thank you for being with me." But the farther Sierra was from her and Simon, the safer she would be. Renae shouldn't have agreed to come here, and she wasn't entirely certain that she had. She'd wanted out of the hospital so that she could take care of Simon...but she hadn't intended for anyone to take care of her.

Especially not a darling little girl who'd already lost her mom.

She couldn't lose her father as well.

She eased away from Sierra and said, "I need to check on Simon." She was the one who was responsible for him. The one who'd nearly lost him because she'd been distracted thinking about a home and a family that she'd decided long ago she couldn't have...not if she wanted to help the kids who needed help, like Faith had needed help.

"I'll go, too," Sierra said, and she scrambled out of bed on the other side, rushed to the door and pulled it open to a tall shadow.

Fear slammed into Renae, and she nearly screamed. But then Sierra said, "Daddy!"

"What are you doing in here?" he asked her. "You're supposed to be in bed."

"I was...with Miss Renae," she replied.

"Your own bed," Clark clarified, but he didn't sound very stern. He stepped back into the hall and pointed toward the stairs, but he was grinning. "I'll be up in a minute to tuck you back in."

"But, Daddy—"

"It's way past your bedtime," he said.

Sierra uttered a dramatic sigh but headed down the hall toward the stairwell.

Renae smiled. "It must be hard to discipline her."

"Discipline?" he asked. "What's that? But don't tell the recruits I said that."

Recruits. "I almost forgot you're a training officer…" She relaxed a little, knowing that he wasn't always in danger on his job. Just now…because he'd helped out her.

"Well, you do have a concussion," he said. "You're liable to forget things."

"Like how I wound up here?" she asked and glanced down at the T-shirt and shorts she was wearing. She didn't remember getting into them, either. They must be his. She was dressed like a recruit now.

"You're the one who wanted to leave the hospital," he said. "Did you forget that, too?"

"No," she said. "I have to take care of Simon."

"You did," he said. "You kept him safe. You fought off the attacker."

"I got knocked out," she reminded him now. "I'm not sure how that was keeping Simon safe. You must have showed up just in time…" Somehow she knew he was the one who'd rescued them.

"And you fighting with the attacker kept him from getting Simon out of the car before I got there," he said. "If you hadn't done that…"

The killer would have gotten the baby out, would have taken him to do what…?

"But he got away?" she asked.

"He?" he asked. "Did you see him? All I saw was a mask. And the gun. And the truck. But I didn't get a good look at any of it with the person firing at me. I fired back, and he or she drove off. What did you see? What makes you think it's a man?"

"Because he was big. And so strong," she said. "I kept hitting him with my laptop, and it didn't even faze him. And then he hit me…" So hard. She reached up to touch her temple and swayed a bit, and Clark was there, his hands on her arms, steadying her.

"You need to sit back down," he said. "You need to lie back down."

But she held on to his arms. Sierra was right. Maybe it was too hard to be alone when you didn't feel well. "Did you see him?" she asked.

He shook his head. "I just saw the dark clothes and the mask. I couldn't tell if it was a man or a tall woman…"

"Bobbi Jo," she murmured.

He shrugged. "I don't know. Tommy's grandma and Hank's mom weren't exactly petite, either. We can't rule anyone out."

"No," she said. "That's why it's so dangerous."

"So let me keep you safe."

"At what cost?" she asked. "Sierra? It's not safe for her if we're here, not with that maniac out there determined to get Simon."

"That maniac was already here," he said. "Slashed the tires on everyone's vehicles but yours."

She gasped.

"He or she must have followed us back here from the bar. There are troopers outside, more than just the one who was here earlier," he said. "We're safe here, probably safer than anywhere else."

But as Renae stared at him, she didn't feel safe. She felt very afraid…of the feelings rushing over her. She could trust him, just like Sierra had told her. She could trust him to keep her physically safe, but what about her heart? Could she trust him with that?

He'd already given his to someone else, to his best friend, and lost her. So maybe Renae was the one he shouldn't trust with his heart…because she'd never intended to settle down, never intended to have a family.

And Clark and Sierra deserved one.

So did Simon…

Clark managed to get Renae to go back to bed. But he couldn't sleep…not with the danger they were all in. Renae was right. It wasn't safe for her to be here, and not just because Ella's killer was on the loose.

It wasn't safe because he was beginning to fall for her…just like Sierra was. He was tucking his daughter in bed now. She'd wanted to go back down to sleep with Renae, but he'd convinced her that Mrs. Potter needed the room, that she was going to share the bed with Renae.

"I miss Mommy," Sierra sleepily murmured.

Pain squeezed his heart. She'd only been a few months old when Ann died, so she didn't really remember her. But she missed having a mom. That longing was probably compounded by watching Mrs. Potter with Renae, and Renae…with everyone. She was so protective, so loving, so fierce, but so determined to do her job.

He leaned over and kissed Sierra's forehead. "I miss Mommy, too," he said.

Ann would have liked Renae. She would have respected her. But she probably wouldn't have chosen her for them. Not after that promise they'd made to each other...

He straightened up and backed out of his little girl's room and into the hall. A creak downstairs had him tensing with fear. He'd assured Renae they were all safe, but the killer had gotten past him and the other trooper earlier today. They'd moved around the driveway completely undetected while they slashed those tires. Like they'd slashed Ella's.

Clark reached for his weapon, keeping his hand on the grip as he headed quietly down the stairs. A shadow moved in the living room and then turned, and Mrs. Potter let out a gasp.

"You scared me," she said.

"Ditto," he said. He studied her for a moment. She wasn't holding the baby. "Where's Simon?" he asked with concern.

"He's sleeping in the nursery. I left the baby monitor down here, though." She held it out to show him. "I'm going to bring it with me so I can hear him while I watch over Renae."

"She was up."

"I know," she said. "I heard you talking...to her and your daughter. Thank you for opening up your home to us. You didn't have to do that."

No. He could have had the troopers stationed at the health department, could have had Renae, her mother and Simon stay there. But the place had already been broken into, and it didn't have a security system. It just hadn't felt as safe to Clark as bringing them here. "I wanted to help. I feel bad that your daughter got hurt earlier today." He should have personally made sure she made it safely back to work. Maybe that was why he'd brought her here, so he could watch over her.

"It's not the first time," Mrs. Potter said with a weary-sounding sigh. "And I'm sure it won't be the last. She's had kids attack her. Moms. Dads. Grand-parents. It's a dangerous job."

It was just confirmation of what he already knew, but dread settled heavily in his stomach at the thought of her being hurt again.

"I wish she would give it up," Mrs. Potter said.

"She can't," Clark said. "She won't…because of Faith."

Mrs. Potter gasped again, like she had when she first saw him in the dark. "She told you about Faith?"

He nodded.

"She never talks about Faith," Mrs. Potter said. "At least not with anyone but me." Tears filled her eyes. "I should have seen it. I was the one who failed Faith, not Renae."

"Her father is the one who failed her," Clark said. "A father is supposed to protect his children, his fam-ily…not hurt them."

He hoped that he wasn't hurting his family by bring-ing Renae and Simon and Mrs. Potter here. He wasn't putting Sierra in just physical danger, but in emotional danger as well—of forming attachments to people who couldn't stay.

They were all inside that house. Was it possible to get close enough, like they had earlier?

If they could, they could end this now…with just a match…

The flame flickered in the darkness of the cornfield.

It would be so easy…

SIXTEEN

Simon was crying. The sound of it drew Renae from her dream. From her nightmare that the killer had gotten inside, had left everyone like he'd left Ella on her kitchen floor...

She jerked fully awake, the horror of that nightmare gripping her, and she realized Simon was really crying, his voice emanating from the baby monitor next to her mom's side of the bed. Phyllis slept soundly, her mouth open, soft snores coming from her. After the drive up and watching the baby, she had to be exhausted.

Renae reached over her mom and grabbed the monitor. Then she quickly slipped out of bed and out of the room. The nursery was upstairs and was probably where Simon was. So she headed up, careful that her bare feet didn't make any noise on the steps. It was early yet, and the first light of day streaked through the many windows of the farmhouse. Everybody else was probably still asleep.

And outside... Hopefully, the troopers that Clark had promised were protecting them were fully awake.

Because she had a feeling that Ella's killer was not giving up.

What was his or her interest in the baby?

He'd stopped crying, and instead of being relieved, alarm struck Renae. Was he okay? She pushed open the door to the nursery and nearly collided with Clark.

He was holding Simon and was bouncing him gently in his arms. Dark circles rimmed his blue eyes, and he looked as if he hadn't slept at all the night before. He stared at her just as intently as she stared at him. "Are you okay?" he asked.

She nodded, and the movement didn't send that shooting pain through her head. The throbbing was just a dull ache now. "Yes. I heard him crying and didn't want him to wake up anyone else."

"I was awake," Clark said.

"Did you sleep at all?" she asked.

He shook his head. "I just kept thinking of all our interviews, trying to figure out who could have killed Ella and gone after Simon like this."

"A monster," Renae said.

"We probably met them yesterday, talked to them," Clark said. "So why can't we figure out which one it is?"

"Lauren could tell us," she said.

"I have troopers searching for her," he said. "She has no credit cards or bank accounts in her name. No way to trace her."

"And if she was stealing money from the restaurant, she might have enough cash to disappear for a while."

"We'll find her," Clark said. "But in the meantime,

you need your rest. Go back to bed, and I'll settle Simon back down. He just needs a diaper change."

"I can do it," she said.

"Sierra just got potty-trained," he said. "So I'm very used to changing diapers." He laid the baby on a changing table and proved that he was far better at it than Renae was. She usually just investigated abuse and placed kids with other relatives or foster care if she found evidence of abuse. She didn't care for the children personally, like she cared for Simon. Everything about this was too personal right now.

"Too bad you're not his father," Renae said. Then the kid would have a family he deserved.

Clark sighed. "Neither Tommy nor Hank wants him, but that might be a good thing."

"Nobody wanting him…?" she asked, her heart aching for the baby…almost yearning for him. But she couldn't want him. Falling for Simon would be just as bad as falling for Clark. She had to resist and focus on finding the baby a proper placement and on finding his mother's killer.

Clark had been awake all night going over those interviews again and again, trying to find some clue of what he'd missed…like he'd missed the killer following them back to his house. He'd put in some calls, too, much to the chagrin of the people he'd woken up. He couldn't help feeling that this was a critical situation. That if the killer wasn't stopped, he was going to kill again.

Simon.

Or Renae.

Pain gripped his heart at the thought of that, of either of them being hurt…or worse. Renae had already been hurt. Her hair covered most of the bandage and the bump on her forehead, but it was there as a reminder of how close she'd come to danger.

How she could have died…

She crossed the room toward him and held out her arms. He wanted to take her into his, wanted to hold her close, but she was reaching for Simon, not him, and as she took the baby from him, some of the tension left her body. She held him close against her.

"So Sierra's not the only one getting attached," he mused.

She tensed and stared up at him, her dark eyes wide with alarm. "I'm—I'm not. I can't…"

"I'm just teasing," he assured her. "I know how much your job means to you."

"Everything," she said. "It's all I ever intend to do."

"No husband? No family of your own?" he asked, and the breath backed up in his chest as he waited for her answer.

She shook her head. "No. It's too hard on the CPS investigators who have families. We have literal deadlines on when we need to make contact with these kids. We can't miss them for birthdays or softball games. And it isn't fair to our families to miss so much." She was staring at Simon when she said it, almost as if she was apologizing to him.

"It would be hard to be married to a CPS investigator," he said. "To know how much danger they are in just doing their job."

Her lips curved into a slight smile. "Like a cop isn't in danger." Her face flushed then. "I'm sorry. I— Your wife—"

"Ann," he said. "We were living in the city when she responded to that call where she was shot. And then I moved out here and transferred to a trainer position."

"You're not training now," she said. "You're in danger because of me."

"Because of a killer," he said. "That was first time someone shot at me. Yesterday. And that day Ann died was the first day someone shot at her. It can be a dangerous job, but yours is more dangerous. You can't carry a gun or even pepper spray."

"It's against protocol," she said.

"It's dangerous," he said, reminding himself as much as her.

"You've been talking to my mother," she mused.

He nodded. "Yes, she's worried about you."

"She wants me to quit," she said.

"I told her that you won't," he said. "That you can't." It would be selfish to ask her to do that for her sake and for all the other Simons out there who needed her help. And maybe to remind himself again, he said, "I can't get involved with someone with a dangerous job. I made a promise to myself and to Ann before she died. If something happened to one of us, we wouldn't take that risk again."

Renae's face flushed. "Are you warning me off?" she asked.

"I'm reminding myself," he said. He was so tempted to make an exception for her, but that wouldn't be fair to Ann, to him or to Sierra. "You are so…"

Beautiful. But it was more than that; she was more than her looks. She was all heart. A beautiful heart. He stepped closer and began to lower his head, needing to kiss her, to see what he was giving up, but before he could make contact, his cell vibrated in his pocket.

It brought him to his senses.

He pulled it out and focused on the screen. It was his captain. "Clark here," he answered.

"Clark, you need to be here," she said. "Come into my office. We got a detective who's able to take over the case, and you need to bring her up to speed."

He felt a twinge of disappointment when he should have been relieved. He was out of his depth on this one. He needed help…to help Renae. The faster the killer was found, the faster she and Simon would be safe.

"I'll be there soon," he said. He clicked off the cell and shared the good news with her.

But she didn't look any happier than he felt. "I should go with you," she said. "Help you fill her in."

He shook his head. "No, you need to rest. The doctor only released you with the promise that you'd be careful and take it easy." And he needed to be careful as well…before he did something stupid like fall for her.

"But still, I know the people—"

"I met them, too," Clark reminded her. "I can bring the detective up to speed."

"Then what?" Renae asked. "Then you'll go back to training recruits? And I'll go back to the health department? I… My mother and I and Simon—we should leave now—"

"We'll figure it out when I get back," he said. "Just go back to sleep for a while. Rest, like the doctor told you to."

Like Clark hadn't been able to because he was so worried. When he left the house a short time later, those fears increased. He couldn't help but think that this was a bad idea, like yesterday, like letting Renae go off alone.

He only hoped that this time she didn't get hurt because of it.

SEVENTEEN

Renae was hurt. Clark had made it pretty clear that he wasn't interested in her, but then he'd almost kissed her.

Or so she thought…

Maybe he hadn't been about to kiss her. Maybe she'd just imagined that.

Maybe she'd just imagined the attraction between them. She looked nothing like Ann. She'd seen her in the wedding portrait on his living room wall, the two of them staring at each other with such love. Ann's hair was a darker blond than Clark's, her eyes a bit darker blue, but her skin was fairer, and her smile so wide and full of happiness.

It wasn't fair that her life had been cut so short. Like Faith's. Like Ella's.

"Just because he loved her, doesn't mean he can't love anyone else," Mom remarked as she joined Renae in front of that picture.

It means he can't love anyone else with a dangerous job.

But she wasn't about to share that with her mother and give her another argument for Renae to quit CPS.

Clark knew and respected her reasons for wanting to devote herself to her career. For Faith...

Just like how he wanted to lead a less dangerous life with a spouse who had a less dangerous career to honor his promise to Ann. That was the right thing for him to do...just as Renae was doing the right thing.

"We should leave," she told her mom. "Go back to the health department building." She needed to get out of Clark's home, out of his life. Right now, he was briefing the detective. He was giving up the case. He shouldn't have to return to such a big part of that case and the danger.

"We can't leave Sierra here alone," her mother pointed out. "He trusted us with her care, and she is the most precious thing in his life."

"She is precious," Renae said. Such a sweet, innocent child. She needed protection, too. "Maybe we can find a number for his aunt or his mother..."

"Renae, why are you so anxious to get out of here?" her mother asked, her gaze intent but soft as she stared at her...as if she knew...or hoped...she knew why.

"I have to find a placement for Simon," she said. "I have to check to see if they rushed the paternity results like Clark requested."

"Clark will let you know—"

"Clark's not going to be handling the case anymore," she interjected, and she felt a twinge of regret over that when she should have been relieved. "A detective is taking over."

"That doesn't mean that you won't have any more contact with him," her mother said.

"But I shouldn't…" Renae murmured. She didn't want this—whatever this was she felt for him—to deepen. Didn't want it to become real.

"Ah, honey, I think he's a really good man, and those aren't easy to find," her mother insisted.

Renae smiled at Phyllis's persistent matchmaking. "Really good men, who've already gone through a loss like his, deserve to be happy. I wouldn't make him happy." She glanced at the wedding portrait again, at the happiness on both faces of the couple. Ann had made him happy. It wasn't fair that he'd lost her.

And he shouldn't have to spend his life worrying about losing anyone else he loved. Not that he loved Renae, but he clearly felt that same…whatever it was… that she was feeling. That attraction or…

Distraction.

That was really what it was. A distraction from what was truly important. Keeping Simon safe and finding his mother's killer.

"What about you?" her mother asked. "Are you happy, Renae?"

She tensed as the question caught her off guard. Normally, she might have brushed it aside and ignored it or answered flippantly. But now she was curious herself, and she stopped to think about it. "I'm happy when there's a good outcome. When I protect a child, when that child is happy, I'm happy."

"You're happy for them," her mother said. "What makes you happy in your personal life?"

"That makes me happy, it truly does," Renae said. "I don't need a personal life."

"You're going to burn out," her mother warned. "You're going to give everything you have to everyone else and have nothing left for yourself. You can do more if you take the time to recharge, if you find someone who will help you and support you with your family, with your emotional well-being."

Renae hadn't considered that before. Hadn't considered having someone at home to give her a hug after a horrible day, someone who would pick up the slack for the missed birthdays and soccer practices.

In her mind, she pictured Clark picking up that slack, offering those hugs. But he'd made it clear she was a risk he wasn't willing to take. And she couldn't deny that after the recent scrapes she'd had that she wasn't in danger. Over the past seven years, she'd had kids kick her, a mother slap her, a dad shake her, but she'd never been run off the road or had someone try to break into a room to get her.

What would this person try next?

Then she heard a gunshot, and she knew.

Please, God, keep us all safe.

Clark knew he shouldn't have gone to the meeting. For one, the detective had been totally disinterested.

"You couldn't handle this?" she'd asked with disdain. "Sounds like a simple domestic situation, ex-husband killed her."

"There's nothing simple about a domestic situation," Clark had remarked with a pang.

"I'm sorry, Clark," his captain said now, her face

flushing as she stared hard at the detective who slouched in one of the chairs in front of her desk. "Clark's wife—"

"That's not what I'm referring to," he said. Losing Ann had also happened because of domestic abuse, because she'd responded to a call about it. Just like Renae had responded to a call, but it hadn't been about domestic abuse. Clark had filled in the detective on his interviews, but he'd found nothing in his notes that suggested anything about this case was simple, and jumping to conclusions certainly wasn't going to help her solve it. "And I can handle it." He had a feeling he could handle it a lot better than this clearly uninterested detective. "I just don't think it's a simple case."

There were so many suspects. So much information missing...

Who was Simon's father? He suspected she'd told Renae the truth, that it was her ex. But then how did Hank figure into things...if at all? And where was Lauren? Was she hurt? Or worse?

Why did someone keep trying to get Simon and for what purpose?

And would they ever give up? Or just keep trying?

He hadn't slept at all the night before because he'd been worried that something might happen. And ever since he'd left his house, he'd been on edge. So on edge that his temper snapped now. "You know, I think I'll just keep this case."

The detective shrugged. "If you think you can close it..."

"I have to close it," Clark said. It was the only way to keep Renae and Simon safe. But even that would only keep Renae safe temporarily. Until the next dangerous case...

If only...

If she'd leave her job, he could see a future with her and even with Simon. But she wasn't interested in adopting the baby or having a husband. And he wasn't interested in someone with a dangerous job. At least, he didn't want to be interested.

"Clark?" his captain asked. "Are you sure? You took the instructor position because you don't want to be out in the field like this, and this case...you've literally brought it home with you."

He released a shaky sigh. "You know how limited resources are in Coral County. We don't have safe houses where we can protect potential witnesses."

"That CPS investigator witnessed something?"

He shrugged. "I don't know if that's why the killer is after her, or if he or she is just after the baby."

"He," the detective insisted. "Simple domestic—"

Clark had had enough of the meeting, had wasted enough time. He turned back to his boss. "I'll update you later today," he said. Right now, he wanted to get back to his house and make sure everyone in it was still safe.

He'd just jumped back into his SUV when the call came in. Shots fired...and the address given by Dispatch was his. All units to respond. And an ambulance. Multiple victims possible.

Multiple...

God, please, no, make sure that they're all unhurt and safe.

Please, God...

He couldn't lose anyone else, not after Ann.

Please, God, they have to be safe...

His boss's office was far enough away from his house that the ambulances beat him there. One sat with its back doors open, paramedics working on someone on a gurney. He rushed out of his SUV to those open doors.

"Who is it? Who's hurt?" he demanded.

One of the paramedics leaned back, and he caught a glimpse of the person on the gurney. Not the face. Just the uniform. The same as his. One of the troopers.

"How bad?" he asked.

"Vest saved him," the paramedic responded. "But broke a rib."

"Any other injuries?" he asked. Any other victims... but he couldn't call them that. Not Sierra or Simon or Renae or her mom. He didn't want to think of them as victims.

"Another trooper."

There had been three. That had left one to protect the house. To protect the people inside...to protect everything in the world that mattered to him. And he wasn't thinking just of Sierra now.

He started toward the house, but now there was more than one trooper there. Two stood at the bottom of the porch steps. One advised him the scene wasn't secure yet.

"It's my house," he said, his voice shaking with fear for them. "I have to go in. I have to see them. Make sure they're all right."

"There's nobody inside, Sergeant," the other trooper said.

"What do you mean?"

The first trooper shrugged. "Two other troopers are searching room by room. But after the shooting stopped, we went inside, and there was nobody there."

He rushed up the steps now, determined to find them. They couldn't all be gone. How would the killer have gotten them all out of the house? Unless there was more than one person involved...

Unless he or she hadn't been working alone this whole time. Maybe the Caufmans didn't just work their restaurant together.

The first trooper had been the one stationed at the house, the only one who hadn't gotten shot. Clark focused on him. "Did you see anyone get inside? Anyone leave?"

The trooper's face flushed. "There were so many bullets flying, and when Williams got hit..." He shuddered with fear. "And then Marty went down, too. And I didn't know where the shots were even coming from. It was chaos."

And frightening. Clark knew that. He'd just had a run-in with the killer the day before where shots had been fired at him. And because of that, it was clear that this killer had no problem taking on law enforcement and trying to take them out.

Had he or she—or they—also taken out all the people who mattered most to Clark?

Where could they be?

Please, God, let them be all right...

EIGHTEEN

"Hide-'n'-seek in the corn is fun!" Sierra exclaimed. Renae wasn't certain if the little girl's voice shook with excitement or fear. "Were those really fireworks...'cause I didn't see 'em..."

That was what Renae had told the little girl the gunshots were. Fireworks. And a signal that the game was starting. The game of hide-and-seek with Daddy's co-workers. Unfortunately, Renae knew where they were. They were lying on the driveway.

Please, God, let them be all right...

Had all of them gotten shot? It had looked like it. When she'd chanced a look out the front windows, the gunfire had been playing out on the driveway. Renae had directed everyone else out the back, through the screen door off the kitchen.

Mom held Simon close to her chest, while Renae carried Sierra. They'd run toward the cornfield, keeping along the edge of it, along a line of trees that cast shadows over the tall stalks and helped to conceal them.

She knew they needed it. Once the gunfire had stopped, she'd heard that back door swing and shut as someone came out looking for them. She'd made Mom move faster, had nearly dragged her along as she carried Sierra.

The little girl had to feel the wild pounding of Renae's heart, the fear gripping her. Hopefully, she thought it was because of the game.

Thank You, God. Thank You for her innocence. Help me protect it and her and Simon and Mom.

Maybe she should have hidden Sierra in the house and kept her out of this. The killer wasn't interested in Clark's daughter. But Renae couldn't leave a vulnerable child in a dangerous situation. Never again...

Stalks snapped behind them as the person gained on them. She urged Mom to move faster, nearly pushing her from behind as she held Sierra closer. Then Simon began to cry, softly at first, and then the cries grew louder.

The noises behind her grew louder as well, as the person stalked them through the field. They were armed. With a gun.

Renae had nothing. She needed a weapon. Needed something...

She nearly tripped over a long tree branch that had fallen from one of those nearby trees. She put down Sierra. "You need to go with Mrs. P and Simon to find a good hiding spot, and I'll catch up with you."

Her mother turned around, her dark eyes full of fear.

"Go, Mom," Renae said, and she picked up that branch. "Go!"

Phyllis was clearly torn, but then Simon cried louder, and she grabbed Sierra's hand and started running.

Please, God, keep them safe.

Please, God, help me keep them safe.

The noise was getting closer, and through the stalks, Renae could see the dark shadow. The black clothes, the mask…the gun…

She wrapped her hands tightly around that branch. Drawing on her softball experience from long ago, she swung the bat as hard and fast as she could. She connected with cornstalks and the person's shoulder. Their grasp on the gun loosened, and it slipped into the mud. Before they could reach for it, Renae swung again, whacking the person's head this time.

A grunt of pain came through that mask. And as the person swayed a bit, Renae dove for the gun. She'd never fired one. Had no idea how. But she dropped her branch to hold it with both hands and direct the barrel toward that killer.

She didn't want to take another life. But she didn't want another life, an innocent life, taken because she did nothing. Before she could squeeze the trigger, the person grabbed the branch she'd dropped and swung it at her.

All Renae cared about now was fighting for her own life and the lives of those innocent children and her mother.

The shot rang out from somewhere inside the corn-field, near the woods. Clark's breath caught when he heard it, and fear gripped him, freezing him in place for a moment. Then he snapped into action, urgency coursing through him as he ran toward that shot. As he did, he noticed the stalks moving in the other direction as someone ran away.

"Stop! Police!" he called out. "Stop!" He couldn't fire, though, not when he couldn't see who it was. He had to find the others. Sierra, Renae, Simon, Mrs. Potter...

Please, God, let them be okay.

Please, God, help me find them.

He looked back now in the direction the shadow had been running from, and he saw her lying back in the mud. "Renae!" he exclaimed and rushed to her side.

Her face was pale but for mud smeared on her cheek, and her eyes were wide with fear. "Did I hit him?" she asked, her voice shaking.

Clark noticed the gun in her hand and the branch lying beside her. He blew out a soft whistle then. "You fought him off..." He wasn't really surprised, not after what she'd done the day before to protect Simon. And now she'd protected Simon and his daughter and her mom. He hoped. "Where are—"

"Renae!" her mom called out, and Simon's cries echoed hers. Even Sierra was crying now.

His heart wrenched in response to his daughter's fear.

"I'm here, Mom," she called back. "And he's gone...?" She glanced toward Clark for confirmation.

He nodded. "You either wounded or scared him away." She was so fierce. So protective...

"Daddy!" Sierra exclaimed and let go of Mrs. Potter to run to him. He caught her up his arms and held her close. "That wasn't fireworks," she murmured, her face buried in his shoulder as her small body trembled against him.

"You're okay," he said. "You're all okay...because of Miss Renae." Something flooded his heart, something more than relief and gratitude. But he ignored it to focus on his daughter.

She pulled back to look down at Renae lying in the mud. "Did you falled down like Grammy?"

"I'm fine," Renae said and forced a smile for his daughter.

Tears stung Clark's eyes as relief overwhelmed him. *Thank You, God.*

He blinked them back and turned toward Renae, using his free hand to help her up from the ground. "And thank you," he said with gratitude.

Tears pooled in Renae's eyes, too, and she was trembling. "I'm sorry," she said.

"Sorry for what?" he asked. "You kept everyone safe." And at the moment, that was all that mattered.

"Those officers..." she whispered.

"They're being treated. Vests protected them. They will be fine." And he had to make sure that they all were as well. He discreetly took the gun from Renae and tucked it into the back of his pants.

Hopefully, it would have a serial number on it that would trace it back to the killer. Hopefully, this would all be over soon, because he wasn't sure his heart could handle any more fear like the fear that had gripped him when he hadn't been able to find his family.

And they all felt like his family now. Not just Sierra...

He'd been worried about his daughter getting too attached, but now he was afraid that he was, too.

That CPS investigator had been a problem from the
very beginning. Now that problem had gotten so bad
that the plan was never going to work. Not that it had
been a well-thought-out plan to begin with...

Disorganized thinking. Wasn't that what the shrink
had called it?

The shrink who'd done nothing to help it.

And now those thoughts jumbled inside the killer's
head, confusing and disjointed and misdirected. Or
maybe it was the cornfield that had done that. Or that
blow that the CPS investigator had delivered...

Maybe that had disjointed the thoughts. The plan.
The plan to get Simon, to keep Simon. To start over...

To make everything better.

But so many people were getting hurt. Maybe
killed...

Had that gun killed anyone? It was gone now, but the
gun hadn't been necessary to get rid of Ella Sedlecky.
And the gun hadn't gotten rid of Renae Potter.

But something would. Something had to...

Because it didn't matter now that everything else had
fallen apart. It was Renae Potter's fault, and she needed
to die for messing everything up.

NINETEEN

Not until her mother locked the door of the nursery with herself and Sierra and Simon inside did any of the tension gripping Renae drain from her body. She'd been so terrified for them. But they were safe now, back at the health department.

There were a couple troopers stationed in the building as well as the security guards she suspected her mother had hired. The state hadn't had enough in their budget to cover them, and the county didn't have anything but this building to offer them for housing. So it was pretty clear the extra security had come from her mom, who was a lawyer, in addition to now being a foster parent. Her dad was a wealthy business owner, and they often shared their wealth with worthy causes. Ever since Faith's death, Phyllis Potter had made certain that the money helped children.

Renae turned toward Clark and apologized, like she'd tried to in the cornfield hours ago. But he shook his head again, rejecting it.

"You have nothing to be sorry about," he said.

"Sierra—"

"Has no idea how much danger you were all in," he said. "You were…" His breath caught, and he stared down at her almost as if he was awed. "You were amazing." He reached out and touched her cheek, sliding his fingers over it. "You are amazing." His gaze dropped to her lips, as if he wanted to kiss her.

Renae wanted him to, so badly, but that guilt refused to leave her, despite his assurances. She didn't deserve his kiss or his compliment. "Clark, I respect how you feel about getting involved with anyone with a dangerous career. After today, after the danger Sierra was in, I totally understand. That must have been your worst nightmare."

"It was," he agreed. "But it wasn't just because of Sierra—"

"Renae!" Her supervisor stood at the end of the hall, near one of the security guards, as if he'd refused to let her past. "You have a call that came through the switchboard for you."

She let out a slight breath, grateful to escape this discussion with Clark and the temptation she'd felt to kiss him.

Just to know what she was missing…

What she could never have. But maybe it was better that she not know. He followed her as she walked toward the cubicle that was her office. There were a few rows of the cubicle offices, but not many of them were used. She rushed toward the phone with the flashing button and picked up the call. "Renae Potter."

"I need your help…" a female voice murmured.

The call reminded her of the one she'd taken just a few short days ago. It seemed more like a lifetime ago. And just like she had then, she asked, "Who is this?"

"Lauren Caufman," the caller replied. "I know you've been looking for me. You and that trooper..."

"Where are you, Lauren?" she asked. "And more importantly, are you and your daughter safe? Are you okay?"

The other woman released a shaky breath. "I don't think so... That's why I need your help."

"Where are you?" she asked again.

"A motel near the interstate," Lauren replied. And she gave the address. Ella hadn't had enough strength left to tell Renae where she was. Lauren had to be okay. But she did sound scared.

"I'll be there shortly," Renae promised.

"Come alone," Lauren said. "I don't want the cop cars here. I don't want anyone else to know where we are."

Renae wasn't going to make that promise...because she had a feeling Clark wouldn't let her keep it. When she hung up and shared the entire conversation with him, he confirmed it.

"You're not going alone," he said. "That sounds like a trap."

"Could Lauren be the one responsible for Ella's death?" she asked with horror.

Was that why she'd disappeared the way she had? Had Ella confronted her about the missing money, as Bobbi Jo had confronted her? She shook her head, silently rejecting Lauren as a suspect. It wasn't possible. While she was tall, Renae didn't think she was as big as the person she'd grappled with in the car or the field. "It couldn't be. The person trying to get Simon out of the car was so much taller and broader."

"Maybe she isn't working alone," Clark suggested. "And that's why you should stay here with your mom and the kids."

Like both kids were hers. But neither were, even though she'd felt like she was protecting her own carlier today, as if Simon and Sierra were her children. The best way to protect them was to stop this killer.

She shook her head. "I need to go. I think Lauren will talk to me—"

"Or try to kill you again," Clark said.

"I really don't think it was her," Renae insisted. "What would be her motive for coming after me? I didn't even investigate the CPS complaint against her, and I know nothing about what was going on at the restaurant. But I think I can get her to tell me what's going on."

He released a low groan of frustration. "You shouldn't go, but you are good at getting people to talk to you…"

"I am," she said.

"I'm afraid she won't be alone when you show up," he said. "But you won't be, either."

A slight smile tugged at her lips. "You're letting me go?"

"I don't think I can stop you," he said.

She figured her mom would try harder, so she didn't tell her she was leaving. Mom would stay here with the kids to make sure nothing happened to them. Keeping Sierra and Simon safe was the most important thing, and the best way to do that was to find who kept putting them in danger. To find who had killed Ella...

Even if it put Renae in danger again to do it.

Everything about Renae amazed Clark. How she'd protected the kids and her mom at his house and in the cornfield. And how even after that traumatic incident and a concussion, she was determined to go out again to meet the woman who'd asked her for help.

He was worried that it was a trick. Maybe Lauren knew that the gun would lead back to her or whoever might be helping her. Wanting to catch Lauren and any potential accomplice, Clark rode in the back seat while Renae drove a state vehicle. Hopefully, that gun was the only one the killer had had access to, or Renae could still be in danger even with him there.

He made her park a few spaces away from the motel room that Lauren had said was hers, and he was careful to stay crouched down below the seats and then between the other guests' vehicles while Renae walked toward the room. He moved around the cars to follow her, to be close when she approached the door.

She reached out and knocked, her hand steady. She wasn't afraid. But he was. The killer shooting at those three troopers had proved how desperate she or he was. Desperate enough to risk getting caught.

Once the door opened, Clark jumped up and stepped in front of Renae, trying to protect her like she'd protected his daughter. And just as he'd worried, Lauren wasn't the one who answered the door.

Greg Caufman stood in the doorway. Clark shoved

him back inside the room. He had his gun drawn, trained on the man. "Put your hands up," he said. "Where I can see them."

Greg hesitated for a moment before he raised them. Then he backed toward the bed, where Lauren sat with her daughter clutched in her arms.

"Are you okay?" Renae asked her. "Has he hurt you?"

"I would never hurt her," Greg protested. "I'm trying to protect her! That's why I brought her here."

"Protect her from whom?" Clark asked.

"From my wife," Greg said. "She's crazy...ever since our son died during basic training, she's lost it. She refuses to accept that he's gone."

"He is?" Renae asked. "Back when she called CPS on Lauren, he was still alive."

"They hadn't confirmed then that he was dead, but he is now," Greg said. "Bobbi Jo won't believe it though. That's why I've been skimming money off the books to give Lauren, to get her and the baby away from Bobbi Jo. But she thought Ella was taking it, and she must've killed her."

"But why go after Simon?" Renae asked. "What would she want with the baby? With me?"

Greg shrugged. "I don't know. Maybe she thinks she can replace our son with Ella's boy."

"She never let me forget how disappointed she was that I had a girl and not a boy to carry on the family name," Lauren said, her arms tightening around her little girl. Then her eyes widened, and she screamed.

Clark whirled around to find Bobbi Jo looming over Renae in the open doorway. Greg stepped back toward

Lauren and his granddaughter, while Clark turned his gun on the woman. But what if she had one, too, and it was trained on Renae? He couldn't see her hands, could only see the rage on her flushed face.

Her look of anger was directed at her husband. "You stupid fool!" she yelled at him. "I knew you were helping her! I knew you were working with her to betray our son!"

"How—how did you find this place?" Greg asked as he worked hard to keep himself between her and Lauren and the baby, as if he was worried, too, that she had a gun.

Bobbi Jo snorted. "There aren't that many motels in the area," she said. "It wasn't hard to check them all."

"Don't hurt us like you did Ella," Lauren pleaded with the woman, tears streaking down her face.

Bobbi Jo snorted again. "I didn't hurt Ella."

"But you thought she was taking the money," Lauren said. "She told me that you accused her of stealing it."

"Is that why you killed her?" Bobbi Jo asked. "So she wouldn't tell me the truth, that you were taking that money to leave my son, to take my grandchild and leave me?"

Lauren's face paled. "I didn't kill her. You did! You're crazy!"

Bobbi Jo's face flushed, and she shook her head. "I'm not crazy. I'm not—"

"You can't face the truth, Bobbi Jo," Greg said almost tentatively. "You can't admit that our son is gone."

She shook her head. "He's not. They made a mistake.

He's not dead. That helicopter was never found. He's alive…" Her voice cracked, and tears filled her eyes.

Clark suspected she knew the truth, but just couldn't bring herself to face it. Right now, he was struggling to figure out what the truth was and which one of them was speaking it.

"Ella Sedlecky definitely isn't alive," he said. "And Miss Potter has nearly been killed and some officers have been shot. We're tracing the weapon that was used." They wouldn't have been able to do that if Renae hadn't gotten the gun away from the killer. "If any of you—"

"We're missing a weapon," Bobbi Jo interjected. "We had a gun behind the bar. Got it after we were robbed ten years ago."

"I know it's missing," Greg said. "I was going to give it to Lauren, but it was already gone. You took it, Bobbi Jo!"

The older woman shook her head. "No. You did. Or you." She pointed at Lauren then. "She's not the sweet innocent you want to believe she is. She tricked our son into marrying her and convinced him to enlist. If he's dead, he's dead because of her! And Ella might be dead because of her, too."

Instead of protesting, Lauren just wrapped her arms more tightly around her daughter, as if she would do anything to protect her. Even kill an innocent woman?

"You knew the gun was there, too," Renae said to her softly.

She nodded. "Ella did, too. She thought one of us should take it because of how crazy Bobbi Jo was act-ing. She thought it was dangerous to leave it there. But she wouldn't have wanted it by her baby. I'm not sure if she took it or not."

Clark doubted it. If Ella had had the gun, she would have used it on whoever had stabbed her. His head pounded harder. "Do you have the registration for it?"

"I thought you were tracing it?" Bobbi Jo challenged him.

"We are," Clark assured her. "We'll find out who it belongs to."

"But you can't prove who used it," Bobbi Jo pointed out, almost as if she knew that nobody would be able to identify her because of that disguise?

"Did you report it missing?" Clark asked.

She narrowed her eyes to glare at him. "Not everybody wants the cops all up in their business. I figured it would turn up eventually."

It had. In a cornfield. Clark wondered if she was the one who'd dropped it there.

"I am all up in your business now," he said. "And I'm not sure any of you are telling the truth. So you're going to go to the local state police post and make official statements." He touched the radio on his collar, calling for reinforcements.

Once another trooper arrived, he left the motel room with the squabbling trio and the crying baby and escorted Renae back to her car. "Another trooper will be here soon, and they can follow you back to the health department building. I'm going to interview them all again at the police post."

"Why do I need a trooper to follow me if it's Bobbi Jo?" she asked. "Isn't it all over now?"

For some reason, Clark didn't feel like it was. Maybe he didn't want it to be. Maybe he didn't want to go back to the training center and have no further contact with Renae.

"I don't know if there's enough to hold her in custody, enough for charges," he said. "But the trooper who just arrived confirmed the gun was registered to Bobbi Jo Caufman."

"She claims it disappeared a while ago," Renae said.

"She doesn't seem too clear on reality right now," Clark said. "Grief can really mess you up. The anger..." He understood all too well how Bobbi Jo could have lost control in her grief.

"But that's no excuse for killing Ella," Renae said. "And why go after Simon? She would have to know that he's not her son. It doesn't make sense." Her brow furrowed as if she was struggling to accept it, too.

"I'll talk to her," Clark said. "I'll see if I can get her to confess."

Renae emitted a sigh. "What a mess..."

Clark nodded. It wasn't just these people who were messed up. He was, too. He'd been so certain that he couldn't risk his heart on someone with a dangerous job. But Renae was so incredible, smart, strong and determined that he was losing his will to resist falling for someone like her, someone whose career put them in peril.

Ann would have respected her. They would have been good friends. And he... He was falling for her like she'd fallen in that muddy field while defending their kids. Their kids. That was how he already felt about Simon.

"Do you think Tommy will change his mind about his son?" he wondered aloud. "Do you think he'll keep him?"

"With Tommy's immaturity and bad attitude, I hope not," she said. "But we don't even have the paternity results back yet."

"You don't think he's Hank's, though?"

She shook her head. "Hank is probably the only one not involved," Renae said. "He's the one who will miss Ella most. Simon won't even remember her."

Like Sierra wouldn't her mother. She couldn't lose another parent. Clark had to stick to his promise even though his feelings for Renae were getting harder and harder to fight. Maybe that was why it was so hard for him to watch her drive away even with that trooper trailing close behind her.

Or maybe he just wasn't comfortable letting her go off without him after all the attempts on her life. Every time that he had, something had happened, and he had a horrible feeling that it might happen again.

But that didn't make sense. They'd probably taken the killer in custody. Unless Bobbi Jo was telling the truth and she hadn't used that gun. But if not her, who?

TWENTY

When Renae braked at a stop sign, she glanced at her work phone and saw the text with the paternity results. Tommy Moore was Simon's father, just as Ella had insisted. Yet she hadn't forced him to support her and their son. She'd let him divorce her.

Had that just been out of pride like Ella had said? Or had there been something more to it? Fear? Or had Ella just thought her son deserved to be loved?

He did. Hopefully, Tommy would sign away his rights to the baby. But then who would take him?

Renae's heart yearned for the baby. But she didn't want a husband and a family. How could she handle a baby on her own? No. Simon deserved more. He deserved someone who would love him completely.

Hank wasn't the father, but he'd been so distraught over losing his best friend. He'd loved Ella. Had he loved her son, too? Would he consider taking the child?

Desperate to find Simon a placement before she did something…like file to adopt him herself, she turned toward Hank's family farm. The trooper was behind her. He would follow and protect her if it was necessary…

But with Bobbi Jo in custody, it shouldn't be necessary. The threat had to be over…as long as a case could be made against the woman. Maybe Ella had told Hank more about the situation with the Caufmans or about the gun. That was another good reason to talk to him again.

When she pulled her vehicle into the driveway, she wasn't certain anyone was there. There were no other vehicles visible, though they could have been shut up in one of the many run-down barns on the property.

That big black truck that had forced her into the ditch could also be in one of them. She wasn't sure why she considered that now…when it seemed pretty obvious that Bobbi Jo was the killer. What possible motive would Hank and his mother have for going after Ella? What would they have gained?

They had no claim on Simon. But maybe that was why the killer was trying to grab him? Because they had no claim on him…

She shook her head with disgust over her own paranoia. Maybe Clark's doubts about the Caufmans telling the truth had made her doubt everyone but him…

She believed him. Her phone dinged with an incoming text from him: Where are you going?

The trooper following her must have updated Clark that she'd veered off from the health department.

She typed in that she was going to the Chester farm and then dropped her phone into her bag. Hank had known Ella best, so maybe he would have some idea about what kind of home she would have wanted her son to have if she couldn't raise him. Or maybe he would want to raise Simon for her.

She stepped out of her car and headed up to the door. The place was really run-down, but that didn't mean as much as love meant. If Hank loved Simon, he would find a way to provide for him like Ella had.

Like Renae could...

While she had money, she didn't have time. Not for a family, and definitely not to be a single mother. If only Clark would reconsider that promise he'd made his wife...

But then Renae would have to reconsider that promise she'd made herself and to Faith's memory.

Her first knock went unanswered. Maybe there were no vehicles in the driveway because they weren't home. She knocked once more before turning to walk away.

The door creaked open behind her. "Miss Potter, what are you doing here?" Mrs. Chester asked. "And why'd you bring the police with you?"

The trooper had stepped out of his vehicle and started toward the porch, but Renae shook her head. "You can stay there," she told him. "I'll just be a couple of minutes."

"Is Hank here?" she asked the woman.

Mrs. Chester hesitated a moment before nodding. "Yes, he's inside just washing up for dinner." She stepped back and held the door open for her. "You can come in."

Renae hesitated now, just a moment, before stepping across the threshold. When the door closed behind her, a sudden chill passed through her. Then Mrs. Chester turned the lock. When Renae turned back toward her, she noticed the heavy makeup on one side of the woman's face. To cover up the scratches and bruises from where Renae had struck her that morning in the cornfield?

"Why'd you lock the door?" Renae asked.

The woman shrugged. "Force of habit, I guess. You must have that, living for as long as you did in the city."

Renae tensed. "How do you know that?"

"Ella must of said something about it…"

"You were close to Ella?" she asked. Close enough that Ella might have called her for a ride that day she found the flat tires? There had been a lot of calls to the landline here at the farm, but Renae had thought Ella was calling Hank.

"She and Hank were friends a long time. I always thought they'd make a cute couple, but she liked the bad boys like that lowlife Tommy Moore."

Some of Renae's tension eased a bit.

"Have a seat," Mrs. Chester said. "And I'll tell Hank you're here."

Renae was exhausted from the traumatic events of the day, so exhausted that her legs shook slightly. She moved quickly toward an easy chair, so quickly that she accidentally kicked over a basket. Blue yarn tumbled out along with a pair of knitting needles. The exact blue yarn of those baby booties from the scene of Ella's murder.

Please, God, help me get safely out of here.

Renae whirled around and headed back to the door, but before she reached out, a hand wrapped around her arm and drew her up short. It was a strong hand. A big hand with calluses on it. Mrs. Chester worked hard on her farm, and that hard work had made her strong.

"You're not going anywhere," Mrs. Chester told her. "Not until I get that baby."

"He's not Hank's," Renae said. "That's what I came to tell your son. That's why I'm here."

"That baby should be his," Mrs. Chester said. "He was supposed to give me grandbabies. A chance to do it better than I did with him. To start over. That's what that baby is. A fresh start. But you ruined it all."

The woman jerked her around to face her, and Renae saw the desperation and madness on her face. Then she saw the hunting knife, the long blade of it already stained with blood. Ella's? Would she have kept the knife?

"If you kill me, you'll never get a chance to see any of your grandbabies," Renae warned her.

"I don't have any grandbabies. I don't have any kids but Hank, and he's never been what I want. Good riddance to him…"

"What happened to Hank? Did you hurt him like you hurt Ella?" If she'd killed her own son, Renae had no chance of escaping her unharmed. She thought of Clark and Simon and Sierra and her mom, and she really wanted to live.

Clark should have heeded his instincts and followed Renae himself. The trooper had let her go into that house alone, and Clark had a feeling that it was a big mistake. He had such a feeling about it that he rushed there with flashing lights and sirens. He was on his way there when the call came from Dispatch…

Stabbing victim at Chester farm on South 46 in Coral County.

Stabbing victim. Panic gripped him, making his foot press harder on the accelerator. He had to get there. Had to see her...

He had to make sure that she wasn't already gone. The stabbing victim had to be Renae. But just in case, he dialed her cell. It rang and rang. Just when he thought voice mail was about to pick up, a female voice answered. "Hello, Sergeant."

It wasn't Renae.

Renae hadn't been able to answer her phone? Because she was hurt?

"Who is this?" he asked.

"Somebody who's very tired of you and Miss Potter getting in my way. If you want to see her again, you need to bring me that baby."

"Why?" he asked. "What do you intend to do with him?"

"I won't hurt him," she replied. "Not like I'm going to hurt Miss Potter if you don't get the baby here right away."

"Is she hurt now?" Clark asked, his heart pounding hard with fear for her. "What have you done to her?"

Please, God, let Renae be okay.

"Bring the baby, and you can find out," the woman replied.

The call disconnected, and he heard the sudden echo of sirens besides his own. An ambulance appeared on the road behind him. He sped up and led it to the farm. As he rolled into the driveway, he saw a man lying on the ground, his clothes stained with blood. He parked, jumped out and dropped to his knees next to the guy.

"Hank," he said, "What happened? What's going on?"

The man coughed, and blood trickled from the corner of his mouth. "I saw the truck...all shot up...and the gun Ella gave me to hide was missing. I figured out..."

"Your mom killed Ella?"

He nodded. "She quit taking her meds. Every time she goes off 'em, she loses it. That's why I grew up in foster homes and at Ella's and her grandpa's. She thinks she can be a mom to Simon...like she never was..." He coughed again, and his eyes started to roll back in his head.

Clark jumped up and out of the way of the paramedics, who rushed to the young man's aid. He hoped they weren't too late, like help had been for Ella.

Please, God...

Tears stung Clark's eyes as emotions overwhelmed him. Once again, Renae was at the mercy of this merciless killer. He had to find a way to get her out. To save her.

The paramedics were applying pressure, inserting IVs, treating Hank. "Wait. I have a question..." He stopped them from lifting the gurney and dropped down beside Hank again. "Can I get inside without her knowing?"

Hank nodded and coughed again before managing in a weak whisper to tell Clark how. It was risky. Everything about his plan was, but it was his only chance to save Renae.

If she was even still alive...

* * *

Through the glass of the front door, Henrietta Chester watched the paramedics lift her son into the back of an ambulance. She should be happy that they were helping him, but he'd been gone so much that it wasn't like he was really even hers. Not anymore…

The baby could be. Another chance. A fresh start.

She could get it right this time. She didn't need Hank. She really didn't need Miss Potter anymore, either. She turned back toward the woman that she'd pushed down into that easy chair next to her knitting basket. Miss Potter had seen the yarn and those booties. She knew.

"See," she said. "I'm going to be the perfect grandma. Going to knit all kinds of stuff for that little guy."

"They're not going to bring him here," Miss Potter said.

Henrietta gripped the knife tighter and started toward her.

"Not if you hurt me," the woman said. "Sergeant Mayweather isn't stupid. He won't hand that baby over to you if I'm dead. He'll want to make sure that I'm okay."

She narrowed her eyes and studied Renae's face. What she was saying made sense…in a way that things sometimes made sense to Henrietta that didn't make sense to other people. "This is your fault, you know," she told her. "You were supposed to take him away from Ella when I called in that complaint. The Moores didn't want no baby, can't take care of him, so you were supposed to look for other people to take him in, people like me and Hank."

"Hank didn't want him, either," Miss Potter said.

She shrugged. "Hank don't know what he wants. Always moving in and moving out. He told Ella about me, made sure she would never even let me watch her kid, said that I was too messed up. He's always trying to get me to take my meds, but they make it even harder to think…" Harder than it already was. Her head throbbed now from where this woman had struck her.

She really wanted to pay her back for that blow. But what if she was right? What if that sergeant wouldn't give her the baby if she killed this woman?

Weren't you supposed to keep hostages alive for the exchange? What you didn't want for what you really did…

But did the sergeant even want this woman? Wasn't that him outside? Was this all falling apart now?

That cell phone, the one she'd taken off the CPS investigator, rang now. She could ignore it, but that wasn't what the hostage taker did in the movies. They picked it up. They negotiated. Like she'd negotiated earlier…

The baby for this woman. She accepted the call, putting it on speaker so she could keep her hands free in case that Potter woman tried anything like she had in the cornfield.

"The baby is here now," Sergeant Mayweather said. "If you look out the front door, you'll see another trooper walking him up the porch."

This is a trick.

Everything suddenly clicked into place for a moment of startling, horrible clarity. They knew she'd stabbed her son. That she'd killed Ella. That she'd gone after this CPS investigator again and again.

They weren't giving her a baby. They were tricking her. And she wasn't going to fall for it. They were coming in. She knew it. They were going to try to arrest her. And she wasn't dying before Miss Potter.

She didn't walk toward the front door like the sergeant wanted. She lifted the knife blade, turned and lunged at the woman.

TWENTY-ONE

Renae knew there was no way that Clark would bring Simon here or let anyone else do it, either, and she saw the moment Mrs. Chester realized it, too. Saw that cloudy look of madness clear from her dark eyes for a moment before she turned and raised the knife and lunged.

Renae was ready. She swung out with the knitting needles she'd surreptitiously picked up from the floor. She hit the woman in the leg, but Mrs. Chester's arms were long, so long that the blade nipped Renae's shoulder. Searing pain shot through it just as a shot rang out.

Mrs. Chester dropped onto the floor. Clark stood over her, his gun drawn, his hands steady on it. But his face was so pale, his eyes so wide and full of fear.

"She got you," he said, pointing his hand toward her wound.

Blood oozed from it, and a sudden buzzing filled Renae's head. It wasn't from the pain, though. The blade hadn't gone that deep, but the wound had affected Clark more than it had her.

It had probably just cemented for him all the reasons why they could never be together. Renae knew those reasons, too. But in that moment, after coming so close to dying, all she wanted was to be with him and Sierra and Simon. All she wanted was to find the happiness her mother had asked if she felt…not just when she closed a case and the kids were happy. But her own personal happiness.

She wanted that now. And she realized her mom was right. She could change her mind. She could figure out a way to balance her work and her life and actually have a life of her own. A love of her own. But she had to accept that she wasn't going to find that with Clark. Because being with him would not make him happy…

In that moment where he saw the blood seeping out of the wound on Renae's shoulder, Clark realized it was too late. He'd already fallen in love with her.

He'd fallen for her fierce spirit. Her determination to save as many kids as she could. And he couldn't ask her not to do that. He just didn't think he was strong enough to have her and lose her like he had Ann. Ann had been his best friend. They'd loved each other, but it hadn't felt like this. Now he understood why they called it falling in love.

He felt like he'd dropped off the edge of a cliff with no ground in sight. He just kept somersaulting through space, unable to grasp anything to stop his descent. And when he finally hit the bottom, it hurt.

Other troopers and paramedics flooded the farmhouse, treating Mrs. Chester and Renae.

Please, God, let her be okay.

Let both of them be okay.

Officers were trained to shoot to kill in situations like this, when they or an innocent person was in imminent danger. But he didn't want to kill anyone, especially someone who just needed help like Mrs. Chester. Since Mrs. Chester was injured the worst, the ambulance took her away first. Renae could have ridden with them, but she rode to the hospital next to him, her shoulder bandaged but still bleeding. Her face was pale but so beautiful.

"Are you okay?" she asked, her voice soft and breaking.

He nearly laughed at the irony of her asking him. "You're the one who's hurt."

"I'm grateful," she said. "I'm grateful that I'm alive."

"Me, too," he heartily agreed.

"You look like you're in more pain than I am," she pointed out.

He glanced into the rearview at his reflection and noticed his face was as pale as hers, but grim as well, his jaw tightly clenched. He sighed. "I am."

"I'm sorry," she said as if she knew it was because of her. "I'm sorry I can't give up my job. I wish I could, but I would feel so guilty, feel like I'm letting down so many people."

"I know," he said. "It's one of the reasons I've fallen for you. That and your fierce   "

She gasped, and now she was the one who looked as if she was in pain. He pressed harder on the accelerator. He needed to get her to the hospital right away.

She reached across the console and grasped his arm.

"I'm sorry," she said again. "I…care too much about you…"

This time, he forced the chuckle and asked, "How can you care too much?"

"I care too much to put you through the fear and uncertainty and maybe even the loss again. You and Sierra have already been through too much. I can't cause you any more pain."

They arrived at the hospital, and as he pulled up to the ER entrance, she pushed open her door. Then she turned back and said, "Don't come inside with me. Just let me go…" She stepped out, slammed the door with her good arm and never looked back as she walked inside.

She was wrong. She'd already caused him more pain. It hurt more to let her go than it had falling for her…

A month passed, and every day, Sierra asked about Miss Renae and Simon and Mrs. P. She asked when they were going to come and stay with them again.

His mom was back to babysitting, her ankle healing nicely. She'd warned him that Sierra wasn't going to let this go, and that he shouldn't, either. He'd fallen in love, and Ann would have wanted that for him. He'd finally shared with her the promise he and Ann had made each other.

Instead of understanding, she'd laughed at him. Pointing to her ankle, she said, "I got hurt watering flowers. Anything can happen anytime, anywhere. You can live in fear of that, and not really live at all. Or you can love with all your might and appreciate every day you have with the people you love."

She was right.

He knew that. And he wanted to tell Renae. But just because he'd changed his mind, didn't mean that she'd changed hers. She'd been determined to never get married, never have a family, never risk letting down a child like she felt she'd let down Faith.

But he called her, anyway. And like the last time he'd called her, another woman answered. "Hello."

"Mrs. Potter?" he asked.

"Yes."

Had Renae had her mother answer her phone for her? Did she not want to talk to him?

"May I speak to your daughter?" he asked.

"She can't come to the phone right now. She's a little busy."

She would always be busy, but he could deal with that. He would appreciate however much of her time she could spend with him and Sierra.

"Where is she?" he asked.

"The courthouse," Mrs. Potter replied.

"Oh, she's testifying…" Testifying in family court was as much a part of her job as the rest of it.

"Not exactly," she said. "But she is making promises of a sort…"

Panic struck him. Was she getting married? He hadn't thought she was even seeing anyone. But he'd let a month go by. A month of silence. He was a fool.

Please, God, don't let me be too late…

"You should come down here," her mother said. "And bring Sierra. And your mother, too. I'd like to meet her."

His head pounded like it had that day when he'd tried to figure out who had killed Ella and he'd had so much information to sort through. This time, he had too little. But before he could ask any questions, she disconnected the call.

"Hey!" he called up the stairs. "We have to hurry! Come on, ladies!"

"Where we goin', Daddy?" Sierra asked as she bounded down the stairs.

"To see Renae," he replied.

"And Simon?"

Renae was at the courthouse. Her mother was there, too, and Renae kept her promises to Faith and to Ella. He realized now how she was keeping that promise to Ella to keep her son safe. She was keeping him.

Moments later, he had confirmation of his suspicion when Renae walked out of the courtroom carrying Simon. She was smiling so widely, looking so happy, that his heart swelled with love for her.

"Miss Renae!" Sierra exclaimed. "And Simon!" She flung her arms around Renae's legs, hugging her tightly. Renae bent down until Sierra could reach the baby and kiss his forehead. He let out a little coo as if he recognized her.

"Congratulations," Clark said.

Renae glanced up at him, and her smile slipped away. "How did you know?" Then she looked over at her mom, who was introducing herself to his. "Oh…"

"She didn't call me," he said in Mrs. Potter's defense. "I called your cell."

"Why?" she asked.

"Because I realized what a coward I was being and wanted to see if I'd blown it with you."

The smile started back, just curving her lips up a little. "Blown what?" she asked.

"My chance to date you."

"I thought I blew it," she said. "When I saw your face after what happened at the Chester farm."

Before he could respond to that, their mothers approached, and with a flurry of chatter, they whisked the kids away, leaving Clark and Renae alone in the courthouse hallway.

"They're probably applying for a marriage license for us," he said.

She nodded. "Probably…"

"How do you feel about that…with how you never want to get married?"

She shrugged. "I've learned that it's okay to change my mind."

"You really adopted Simon?" he asked, his heart overflowing now with love and admiration for her.

She nodded. "I made a promise to Ella."

"You saved her son and kept him safe," he said.

"I want him to be happy, too," she said. And then she stepped a little bit closer to Clark and tilted up her head. "I want to be happy, too."

He smiled down at her. "What would make you happy, Miss Renae?"

"Simon," she replied.

He tensed for a moment, worrying that he had blown it.

"And you and Sierra," she added. Then she rose up on tiptoe and kissed him.

He felt that jolt of awareness, that tingly sensation that brought him to life again. To love again…

* * * * *

Get 3 FREE REWARDS!

We'll send you 2 FREE Books <u>plus</u> a FREE Mystery Gift.

FREE Value Over **$20**

Both the **Love Inspired®** and **Love Inspired® Suspense** series feature compelling novels filled with inspirational romance, faith, forgiveness and hope.

YES! Please send me 2 FREE novels from the Love Inspired or Love Inspired Suspense series and my FREE gift (gift is worth about $10 retail). After receiving them, if I don't wish to receive any more books, I can return the shipping statement marked "cancel." If I don't cancel, I will receive 6 brand-new Love Inspired Larger-Print books or Love Inspired Suspense Larger-Print books every month and be billed just $6.49 each in the U.S. or $6.74 each in Canada. That is a savings of at least 16% off the cover price. It's quite a bargain! Shipping and handling is just 50¢ per book in the U.S. and $1.25 per book in Canada.* I understand that accepting the 2 free books and gift places me under no obligation to buy anything. I can always return a shipment and cancel at any time by calling the number below. The free books and gift are mine to keep no matter what I decide.

Choose one:
☐ **Love Inspired Larger-Print** (122/322 BPA GRPA)

☐ **Love Inspired Suspense Larger-Print** (107/307 BPA GRPA)

☐ **Or Try Both!** (122/322 & 107/307 BPA GRRP)

Name (please print)

Address   Apt. #

City   State/Province   Zip/Postal Code

Email: Please check this box ☐ if you would like to receive newsletters and promotional emails from Harlequin Enterprises ULC and its affiliates. You can unsubscribe anytime.

Mail to the Harlequin Reader Service:
IN U.S.A.: P.O. Box 1341, Buffalo, NY 14240-8531
IN CANADA: P.O. Box 603, Fort Erie, Ontario L2A 5X3

Want to try 2 free books from another series? Call 1-800-873-8635 or visit www.ReaderService.com.

Get 3 FREE REWARDS!

We'll send you 2 FREE Books plus a FREE Mystery Gift.

FREE Value Over **$20**

Both the **Harlequin® Special Edition** and **Harlequin® Heartwarming™** series feature compelling novels filled with stories of love and strength where the bonds of friendship, family and community unite.